The Brain Blueprint:

Unlocking Optimal Health with Nutrition, Herbs, Acupressure, and Beyond

By

Dr. JOHN JUNG

Table of Contents

Introduction:

Your brain is the command center for every thought, emotion, and movement. Yet, in today's fast-paced world, many of us unknowingly compromise its health—whether through poor nutrition, stress, or environmental factors. The Brain Blueprint unveils a comprehensive approach to nurturing cognitive function, emotional balance, and mental clarity by addressing vital components such as nutrition, herbs, acupuncture, hormones, lifestyle changes, vitamins, homeopathy, minerals, nootropics, and amino acids.

In these pages, you'll discover how to assess imbalances that may be impacting your focus, memory, and overall well-being. Using scientifically backed methods and holistic wisdom, this book will guide you toward effective testing strategies to identify deficiencies and excesses. Armed with this knowledge, you can tailor interventions to optimize brain health, enhance performance, and cultivate lifelong resilience.

Whether you're seeking to sharpen your mind, recover from mental fatigue, or simply gain a deeper understanding of the brain's intricate workings, The Brain Blueprint is your guide to achieving lasting cognitive vitality.

Why this book?

In 2015, my 15-year-old daughter was going through some hormonal changes and acting irrationally. I brought her to a local hospital to be observed for 24 hours. The psychiatrist at the time put her on drugs without parental consent, and I was not notified. When I learned of this and tried to take her out, they threatened me with the police. She was not harmful to herself or others. I managed to contact administration and got her released, as no diagnosis was made, and the psychiatrist left the hospital the next day, as I was going to file charges. He actually left the country within a week. No joke.

A second example was a lady friend with a bad drinking problem. I acted as the primary doctor and contact. I got a call from the staff the next day—she was given Haldol, a drug that can cause permanent robotic movements, without notifying me. I had her transferred to another rehab center, and it took a while to remove the "Haldol shuffle," noticed by the staff and other patients who saw her turn into a "zombie." Again, I had to personally intervene and threaten the hospital, since I was not informed as her primary contact and doctor.

These are not isolated examples of mismanaged mental care. It happens more frequently than you think.[1]

"First Do No Harm" is a 1997 American drama television film directed by Jim Abrahams and starring Meryl Streep. The story follows Lori Reimuller, a mother whose young son, Robbie, is diagnosed with severe epilepsy. As his condition worsens, traditional medications fail to

---

[1] https://www.youtube.com/watch?v=T0Y2gGk6jEw

control his seizures and cause serious side effects, including Stevens–Johnson syndrome.

Desperate for a solution, Lori discovers the ketogenic diet, an alternative treatment that has helped some epilepsy patients. However, she faces resistance from the medical establishment and the schools, demanding they will take her child away unless she agrees to surgical or continuing pharmaceutical treatments. Determined to help her son, Lori fights against the system to give Robbie a chance at recovery through dietary therapy.

The film is based on real-life experiences and highlights the struggles families face when seeking alternative medical treatments. It was critically acclaimed, earning Meryl Streep nominations for a Primetime Emmy Award and a Golden Globe Award. Basically, using the keto diet as developed in the '20s by the Mayo Clinic.

The ketogenic diet was first introduced by Dr. Russell Wilder at the Mayo Clinic in 1921, not 1902. Wilder coined the term "ketogenic diet" and proposed it as a treatment for epilepsy, mimicking the effects of fasting by shifting the body's energy source from glucose to fat. This is BEST for the brain.

"Maybe I'm possessed?"

In my work with deeply religious clients, I've often encountered moments where behaviors seem almost beyond explanation. Stepping into a mental health facility, I can't deny that some individuals exhibit actions that could be mistaken for something supernatural. But where do we draw the line?

Religious traditions have long sought to differentiate between spiritual disturbances and mental illness, though the approaches vary widely. The Catholic Church, for example, does not rely on blood chemistry to diagnose demonic possession. Instead, it employs rigorous discernment, often requiring medical and psychiatric evaluations before an exorcism is considered. According to the Catechism, distinguishing between mental illness and demonic activity is essential, with medical treatment falling within the realm of science.

Exorcists assess cases based on signs such as inexplicable knowledge, speaking unknown languages, or demonstrating extraordinary physical strength. The Vatican has even hosted seminars to help clergy and laypeople differentiate between psychiatric conditions and spiritual afflictions—though no blood tests or neurological assessments are involved.

Islamic exorcism, known as ruqya, focuses on spiritual healing through Quranic recitation to expel negative influences. While some scholars acknowledge mental health conditions, traditional exorcists often attribute symptoms like hallucinations or erratic behavior to supernatural causes rather than neurochemical imbalances. Similarly, in Jewish Kabbalistic traditions, exorcisms have historically involved prayers, fasting, and invoking divine names rather than scientific analysis.

Modern religious communities increasingly recognize medical and psychological perspectives, understanding that disorders like schizophrenia or epilepsy may have neurological origins. However, faith-based interventions remain the primary approach for exorcists—none of whom rely on brain chemistry assessments.

That said, science has shown that specific changes in neurotransmitters can contribute to behaviors that may be mistaken for possession:

- **Dopamine Dysregulation:** Excess dopamine activity can lead to hallucinations and delusions, frequently seen in schizophrenia and certain drug-induced states.

- **Serotonin Imbalance:** Low serotonin levels may contribute to mood instability, impulsivity, and aggression.

- **Glutamate Dysfunction:** Abnormal glutamate signaling is linked to dissociative states and psychotic symptoms, affecting one's sense of reality.

- **GABA Deficiency:** Reduced GABA activity can heighten anxiety, paranoia, and involuntary movements, sometimes resembling convulsions or trance-like states.

- **Substance-Induced Changes:** Psychoactive drugs can drastically alter brain chemistry, leading to experiences reminiscent of possession.

Historically, conditions such as epilepsy, schizophrenia, and dissociative identity disorder have been misinterpreted as supernatural afflictions. Today, a neurocognitive evaluation can provide some insight into whether psychiatric or neurological factors are at play.

But the question remains—should any diagnosis be made without biological testing?

If a diagnosis is correct, what is the ideal treatment when individuals respond differently?

Does that mean their condition stems from a lack of drugs?

Prescribing medication without assessing metabolites and toxins raises concerns. Faith healing, without physiological testing, operates under a similar uncertainty. In both cases, the absence of thorough biological evaluation leaves critical gaps in understanding.

50% of people taking antianxiety and antidepressants get no results. Yet we all know someone on them. This book will explain what can be done. Doctors handing out pills before actually doing lab testing should be disciplined, in my opinion. They will tell you Ambien, clonazepam, and Valium are all addictive, and don't like to prescribe them, even though most of my patients had insomnia as a leading cause to visit. But antidepressants are handed out like candy; they too have huge withdrawal and addiction properties. It doesn't make sense to me.

This is from WebMD: Antidepressants can be effective for managing depression and anxiety, but they may come with side effects.

- Nausea – Often occurs when starting medication but may improve over time.

- Weight gain – Some antidepressants can increase appetite or affect metabolism.

- Trouble sleeping – Insomnia or excessive drowsiness can be side effects.

- Dry mouth – Reduced saliva production can lead to discomfort.

- Blurred vision – Some medications may temporarily affect eyesight.

- Dizziness – Feeling lightheaded or off-balance.

- Anxiety – Some people experience increased nervousness initially.

- Headache – A common side effect that may lessen over time.

- Diarrhea or constipation – Digestive issues can occur.

- Sexual problems – Reduced libido or difficulty with arousal.

- Fatigue – Feeling unusually tired or sluggish.

- Tremors – Shaking or involuntary movements.

- Increased sweating – Some medications cause excessive perspiration.

Other serious side effects may include low sodium levels, bleeding risks, and suicidal thoughts, particularly in younger individuals.

- Research on antidepressants for teenagers has examined their effectiveness and tolerability, "but long-term impacts on future medication use are still being studied."[2]

Most adolescents are in the phase of development and growth, and the 5-Hydroxytryptamine (5-HT) and norepinephrine neurotransmitter systems in the nervous system are not yet mature. The response to antidepressants is different from that of adults.

The Citizens Commission on Human Rights International (CCHR) published a report in March 2018 discussing the potential link between psychotropic drugs and mass shootings. The report, titled Psychiatric Drugs Create Violence & Suicide: School Shootings & Other Acts of

---

[2] *Comparative efficacy of antidepressant medication for adolescent depression: a network meta-analysis and systematic review. BMC Psychiatry 25, 471 (2025). https://doi.org/10.1186/s12888-025-06941-x*

Senseless Violence, presents over 30 studies that examine the effects of antidepressants, antipsychotics, and other psychiatric medications on aggression, hostility, and suicidal thoughts.*

Antidepressant medication success varies depending on the type of drug and the individual. Studies show that antidepressants are sometimes effective, but not universally so.

- Selective serotonin reuptake inhibitors (SSRIs) (like Prozac, Zoloft, and Lexapro) are often the first-line treatment. They work better than placebo for most people, but effectiveness varies.

- Serotonin and norepinephrine reuptake inhibitors (SNRIs) (like Cymbalta and Effexor) may be more effective for some individuals, but they tend to have more side effects.

- Atypical antidepressants (like Wellbutrin) work differently and may be better suited for certain cases.

- A major review found that some antidepressants—such as escitalopram, paroxetine, sertraline, agomelatine, and mirtazapine—were more effective and better tolerated than others.

Overall, about 30–50% of people may still experience symptoms even while on medication, and some may need additional treatments. That's the best they can do, with side effects from the medications, including suicidal thoughts in the first month, especially under 25 years of age.

Serotonin syndrome is a potential side effect that can cause a range of physical and mental symptoms, varying from mild to severe. Serotonin syndrome can occur at therapeutic doses, increased doses, or when multiple serotonergic drugs are combined. There is no single threshold dose that universally triggers serotonin syndrome, as individual sensitivity varies.

Physical Symptoms

- High fever and excessive sweating
- Rapid heart rate and high blood pressure
- Muscle rigidity, tremors, or twitching
- Dilated pupils and abnormal eye movements
- Shivering or goosebumps
- Diarrhea and nausea
- Seizures (in severe cases)

Cardiovascular & Metabolic Diseases

- Heart Disease – Chronic stress and depression increase inflammation and blood pressure.
- Diabetes – Anxiety and depression can worsen blood sugar control.
- Hypertension – Stress cont GUT-BRAIN AXISributes to high blood pressure.
- Obesity – Emotional eating and stress hormones can lead to weight gain.

Mental Symptoms

- Agitation or restlessness
- Confusion or disorientation
- Hallucinations or delirium
- Anxiety or panic attacks

Loss of consciousness (in extreme cases)

(Combining St. John's Wort with certain antidepressants, especially Selective Serotonin Reuptake Inhibitors (SSRIs), can lead to serotonin syndrome—a potentially life-threatening condition caused by excessive serotonin levels in the brain.)

What are the Medical FACTS?

The number needed to treat (NNT) for antidepressants varies depending on the type of medication and the severity of depression. For selective serotonin reuptake inhibitors (SSRIs), the NNT is 7, meaning that seven patients need to be treated for one additional patient to experience a significant improvement compared to placebo. For tricyclic antidepressants (TCAs), the NNT is 9. You are wasting your life taking this crap!

Mental health

Mental health can significantly impact various physical diseases, either by worsening symptoms or increasing susceptibility to illness. Here are some conditions where mental health is an aggravating factor:

Gastrointestinal & Gut Disorders

- Irritable Bowel Syndrome (IBS) – Anxiety and stress can trigger symptoms.

- Leaky Gut Syndrome – Mental health imbalances may contribute to gut permeability.

- Crohn's Disease & Ulcerative Colitis – Stress can worsen inflammation.

Neurological & Autoimmune Disorders

- Multiple Sclerosis (MS) – Stress and depression can worsen flare-ups.

- Parkinson's Disease – Anxiety and depression may accelerate cognitive decline.

- Alzheimer's & Dementia – Chronic stress may contribute to neurodegeneration.

- Lupus – Emotional distress can trigger autoimmune flare-ups.

- Fibromyalgia – Anxiety and depression can intensify pain sensitivity.

Chronic Pain & Inflammatory Conditions

- Arthritis – Depression and stress can increase inflammation and pain perception.

- Migraines – Anxiety and stress are common triggers.

- Chronic Fatigue Syndrome (CFS) – Mental health struggles can worsen fatigue.

Hormonal & Endocrine Disorders

- Thyroid Disorders (Hypothyroidism, Hashimoto's) – Depression and anxiety can exacerbate symptoms.

- Adrenal Fatigue – Chronic stress depletes adrenal function.

- Polycystic Ovary Syndrome (PCOS) – Anxiety and depression may worsen hormonal imbalances.

The GUT-BRAIN AXIS

The GUT-BRAIN AXIS is a complex communication network linking the gut and the brain, playing a crucial role in mental health. Research suggests that depression and anxiety may be influenced by imbalances in gut microbiota, inflammation, and neurotransmitter production.

A recent study on depression and anxiety was characterized by an enrichment of pro-inflammatory bacteria and a depletion of anti-inflammatory SCFA-producing bacteria. Specifically, Actinobacteria, Proteobacteria, Rikenellaceae, Porphyromonadaceae, and Bifidobacteriaceae were more abundant in the depression group, while Firmicutes, Prevotellaceae, and Ruminococcaceae were in lower abundance. In the anxiety group, the abundance of Firmicutes, Lachnospira, Faecalibacterium, Sutterella, and Butyricicoccus was lower, while the abundance of Bacteroidetes, Enterobacteriaceae, and Fusobacterium was increased.[3]

Psychobiotics are certain probiotic strains that have shown promise in supporting mental health by influencing the gut-brain axis. Here are some of the most effective strains:

- Lactobacillus rhamnosus – Known for reducing anxiety and stress.

- Bifidobacterium longum – Helps improve mood and cognitive function.

---

[3] Cao, Y., Cheng, Y., Pan, W. et al. Gut microbiota variations in depression and anxiety: a systematic review. *BMC Psychiatry* 25, 443 (2025). https://doi.org/10.1186/s12888-025-06871-8

- Lactobacillus helveticus – Shown to alleviate symptoms of depression.

- Bifidobacterium bifidum – Supports gut health and may reduce inflammation.

- Lactobacillus acidophilus – Plays a role in neurotransmitter production.

- Saccharomyces boulardii – A beneficial yeast that supports gut balance.

- Bifidobacterium infantis – Helps regulate immune responses and inflammation.

- Lactobacillus plantarum – May improve stress resilience.

- Bifidobacterium lactis – Supports overall gut health and mood regulation.

- **SCFA** – Some supplements provide butyrate, a key SCFA for gut health, as well as fiber and fermented foods. This is a must for anybody.

How the Gut-Brain Axis Relates to Depression & Anxiety

1. **Microbiota & Neurotransmitters**
   - The gut houses trillions of bacteria that help produce neurotransmitters like serotonin, dopamine, and GABA, which regulate mood and stress.
   - Dysbiosis (an imbalance in gut bacteria) can lead to reduced serotonin levels, contributing to depression and anxiety.

2. **Inflammation & Stress Response**
   - Gut bacteria influence the immune system, and an unhealthy gut can trigger chronic inflammation, which has been linked to depression.

- The hypothalamic-pituitary-adrenal (HPA) axis, which controls stress responses, is affected by gut microbiota. Dysregulation can lead to heightened anxiety.

3. **Gut Permeability & Brain Function**

   - A compromised gut barrier (often called leaky gut) allows harmful substances to enter the bloodstream, potentially affecting brain function and mood.

   - Certain gut bacteria produce short-chain fatty acids (SCFAs) that support brain health, but imbalances can reduce their protective effects.

Potential Solutions

- **Probiotics & Prebiotics:** Can help restore gut microbiota balance and improve mood.

- **Dietary Changes:** A diet rich in fiber, fermented foods, and omega-3s may support gut and brain health.

- **Stress Management:** Practices like meditation and exercise can positively influence the gut-brain axis.

- **Stop sugar!**

Probiotics & Prebiotics (Balance gut bacteria)

- Probiotics (Lactobacillus, Bifidobacterium strains): 10–50 billion CFU per day

- **Prebiotics** (Inulin, FOS, GOS): 2–10 grams per day

Herbal & Adaptogenic Supplements (Reduce stress & inflammation)

- Ashwagandha: 300–600 mg per day

- Rhodiola Rosea: 200–600 mg per day

- Chamomile: 400–1,500 mg per day

Essential Nutrients (Support brain & gut health)

- Omega-3 Fatty Acids: 1,000–3,000 mg per day
- Magnesium: 200–400 mg per day
- Vitamin D: 1,000–4,000 IU per day
- Zinc: 10–30 mg per day

Neurotransmitter Precursors (Enhance mood & cognitive function)

- L-Theanine: 100–400 mg per day
- 5-HTP: 50–300 mg per day
- SAM-e: 400–1,600 mg per day

NOOTROPICS

Nootropics, often called "smart drugs," are substances that enhance cognitive function, memory, focus, and overall brain health. They can be natural or synthetic, each with different mechanisms and recommended dosages. Here are some common nootropics and their typical dosages:

Common Nootropics and Dosages

Natural Nootropics

- Bacopa Monnieri: 300–500 mg per day
- Lion's Mane Mushroom: 500–3,000 mg per day
- Ginkgo Biloba: 120–240 mg per day
- Rhodiola Rosea: 200–600 mg per day
- Ashwagandha: 300–600 mg per day

Synthetic Nootropics

- Piracetam: 1,200–4,800 mg per day

- Aniracetam: 750–1,500 mg per day

- Modafinil: 100–200 mg per day

- Noopept: 10–30 mg per day

- Phenylpiracetam: 100–200 mg per day

  Cholinergics (Boost Acetylcholine)

- Alpha-GPC: 300–600 mg per day

- Citicoline: 250–500 mg per day

- Huperzine A: 50–200 mcg per day

Several genes have been linked to anxiety and depression, including **MTHFR**, which affects folate metabolism and neurotransmitter production. Other genes that may play a role include:

- **COMT**: Influences dopamine breakdown, affecting mood and stress response.

- **MAO-A**: Regulates neurotransmitters like serotonin and dopamine, impacting emotional stability.

- **GAD1**: Involved in GABA production, which helps regulate anxiety.

- **BDNF**: Supports brain plasticity and resilience, with lower levels linked to depression.

- **5-HTTLPR (SLC6A4)**: Affects serotonin transport, influencing susceptibility to anxiety and depression.

Genetic variations in these genes can contribute to mental health challenges, but environmental factors, lifestyle, and personal experiences also play a significant role.

MTHFR, short for **methylenetetrahydrofolate reductase**, is a gene that plays a crucial role in folate metabolism. Folate is a B vitamin that is essential for numerous bodily functions, including DNA synthesis and repair, as well as neurotransmitter production. Mutations in the MTHFR gene can lead to a wide range of health issues, both mental and physical. Mental health problems associated with MTHFR mutations include depression, bipolar disorder, schizophrenia, ADHD, and autism.

Physically, these mutations are linked to cardiovascular disease, stroke, and osteoporosis. Earlier studies have shown a possible link between MTHFR mutations and various psychiatric disorders, suggesting that these genetic variations can significantly impact mental health.

Studies on **methylfolate (MTHF)** for anxiety suggest that it can be beneficial, especially for individuals with MTHFR gene mutations, which affect folate metabolism and neurotransmitter production. However, exact success rates vary.

Up to 50% of people may have an MTHFR mutation that impacts mental health. The most common variants are **C677T** and **A1298C**, which can affect folate metabolism and methylation processes. The prevalence varies by ethnicity, with Hispanic individuals being more likely to have the C677T variant compared to other groups, according to the CDC.

- Some research indicates that methylfolate supplementation can improve mood and anxiety symptoms, but there isn't a universally agreed-upon percentage of people who experience full relief.

- The effectiveness depends on individual genetics, diet, and overall health.

- I find it almost always works, especially in women!

How to check it?

Methylation Panel

Here are some sources where you can purchase methylation panels:

- Genova Diagnostics – Offers a comprehensive methylation panel that assesses methylation metabolites and genetic SNPs.

- **MaxGen Labs** – Provides the MaxFunction Panel, which tests for 100 genetic variations related to methylation, detoxification, and neurotransmitter balance.

- **DHA Laboratory** – Sells a methylation panel that combines biomarkers with genetic information for a complete assessment.

- https://geneticgenie.org/methylation-analysis/ – where you can upload raw data from AncestryDNA, 23andMe, MyHeritage, FTDNA, Living DNA, HomeDNA, WeGene, 23Mofang, and others, or upload a whole genome sequencing file. Cost: $10–$25.

For individuals with confirmed MTHFR mutations, it's often recommended to take methylated forms of B6 (P-5-P) and B12 (methylcobalamin) since these are more bioavailable and can bypass the impaired methylation pathway.

- **Methylcobalamin (B12)**: Supports homocysteine metabolism and neurological function.

- **Pyridoxal-5-Phosphate (B6)**: Assists in neurotransmitter production and methylation processes.

- **L-Methylfolate (Active Folate)**: The bioavailable form of folate crucial for methylation.

These forms are typically more effective for those who struggle with homocysteine regulation due to MTHFR mutations.

Recommended Dosages

Methylated B12 (Methylcobalamin)

- General dosage: 1,000–5,000 mcg per day

- Higher therapeutic doses: Up to 10,000 mcg per day (under medical supervision)

Methylated B6 (Pyridoxal-5-Phosphate, P-5-P)

- General dosage: 20–100 mg per day

- Higher therapeutic doses: Up to 200 mg per day (under medical supervision)

Popular Brands

Methylated B12

- Jarrow Formulas Methyl B12

- Pure Encapsulations Methylcobalamin

- Seeking Health Active B12

- Thorne Research Methylcobalamin

Methylated B6 (P-5-P)

- NOW Foods P-5-P

- Pure Encapsulations P-5-P

- Thorne Research Pyridoxal 5'-Phosphate

- Seeking Health P-5-P

Anxiety Treatment & Recommended Dosages

Herbal Remedies

- Ashwagandha: 300–600 mg per day

- Chamomile: 400–1,500 mg per day

- Passionflower: 200–400 mg per day

- Lemon Balm: 300–600 mg per day

- Valerian Root: 400–900 mg per day

Amino Acids & Neurotransmitter Support

- L-Theanine: 100–400 mg per day

- 5-HTP: 50–300 mg per day

- GABA: 250–750 mg per day

Minerals & Vitamins

- Magnesium: 200–400 mg per day

- Vitamin B Complex: Dosage varies by individual needs

- Omega-3 Fatty Acids: 1,000–3,000 mg per day

Bipolar Disorder – Typical Dosages

Omega-3 Fatty Acids

- Dosage: 1,000–3,000 mg per day
- Benefits: May help reduce mood swings and stabilize emotions.

Magnesium

- Dosage: 200–400 mg per day
- Benefits: Supports relaxation and may help with anxiety and irritability.

N-Acetylcysteine (NAC)

- Dosage: 600–2,400 mg per day
- Benefits: May help reduce depressive symptoms and improve mood regulation.

Lithium Orotate (Natural Alternative to Prescription Lithium)

- Dosage: 5–20 mg per day
- Benefits: Helps stabilize mood and reduce manic episodes.

Rhodiola Rosea

- Dosage: 200–600 mg per day
- Benefits: Supports stress resilience and may help with depressive symptoms.

Ashwagandha

- Dosage: 300–600 mg per day

- Benefits: Helps regulate cortisol and reduce stress-related mood fluctuations.

St. John's Wort

- Dosage: 300–900 mg per day

- Benefits: May help with mild to moderate depression (but should be used cautiously due to interactions with medications).

SAM-e

- Dosage: 400–1,600 mg per day

- Benefits: Supports neurotransmitter function and mood balance.

Vitamin D

- Dosage: 1,000–4,000 IU per day

- Benefits: Deficiency is linked to mood disorders, including bipolar disorder.

B Vitamins (B6, B12, Folate)

- Dosage: Varies by individual needs

- Benefits: Supports brain function and neurotransmitter production.

Depression – Typical Dosages

Herbal Remedies

- St. John's Wort: 300–900 mg per day; I have some people on 5,000 mg

- Rhodiola Rosea: 200–600 mg per day

- Saffron: 30 mg per day

- Ashwagandha: 300–600 mg per day

- Chamomile: 400–1,500 mg per day

Amino Acids & Neurotransmitter Support

- 5-HTP: 50–300 mg per day

- L-Tryptophan: 500–2,000 mg per day

- SAM-e: 400–1,600 mg per day

Vitamins & Minerals

- Omega-3 Fatty Acids: 1,000–3,000 mg per day

- Vitamin D: 1,000–4,000 IU per day

- Magnesium: 200–400 mg per day

- B Vitamins: Dosage varies by individual needs

- Zinc: 10–30 mg per day

Transcranial Magnetic Stimulation (TMS) is an emerging treatment for depression:

- Standard rTMS: Response rates range from 30–60%, with remission rates around 30%.
- fMRI-guided TMS (SAINT protocol): Shows higher success rates, with 79% remission in some studies.

- **Accelerated TMS**: Emerging research suggests faster symptom relief, sometimes within one week.

- TMS can be performed on either the left or right side of the brain, depending on the treatment approach. Traditionally, left-sided TMS is more common and uses high-frequency stimulation to activate the left dorsolateral prefrontal cortex (DLPFC), which is often underactive in depression.

- Right-sided TMS is also used, particularly for patients who experience both depression and anxiety. It applies low-frequency stimulation to the right DLPFC, which tends to be overactive in these conditions. Some treatment strategies even involve bilateral TMS, stimulating both sides.

Electroconvulsive Therapy (ECT)

- Success rate: Around 50–80% for severe depression.

- Used for: Treatment-resistant cases, but may have cognitive side effects.

Transcranial Direct Current Stimulation (tDCS)

- Success rate: Lower than TMS, with response rates around 20–40%.

- Used for: Mild to moderate depression.

Other Specific Conditions

Adrenal Fatigue

Vitamins & Minerals

- Vitamin C: 500–2,000 mg per day – Supports adrenal hormone production.

- Magnesium: 200–400 mg per day – Helps regulate stress response.

- B Vitamins (B5, B6, B12): Dosage varies – Essential for energy and adrenal health.

Adaptogenic Herbs (Help balance cortisol levels)

- Ashwagandha: 300–600 mg per day – Reduces stress and supports adrenal function.

- Rhodiola Rosea: 200–600 mg per day – Enhances resilience to stress.

- Holy Basil (Tulsi): 300–600 mg per day – Helps regulate cortisol.

- Licorice Root: 400–1,200 mg per day – Supports adrenal hormone balance.

- Maca Root: 1,500–3,000 mg per day – Helps with energy and hormone regulation.

Amino Acids & Neurotransmitter Support

- L-Tyrosine: 500–2,000 mg per day – Supports dopamine and adrenal function.

- Glycine: 500–3,000 mg per day – Helps with relaxation and stress reduction.

Healthy Fats & Nutrients

- Omega-3 Fatty Acids: 1,000–3,000 mg per day – Supports brain and adrenal health.

- CoQ10: 100–300 mg per day – Helps with energy production.

Thyroid Dysfunction

Thyroid dysfunction and anxiety and depression have a well-documented connection. The thyroid gland plays a crucial role in regulating metabolism, energy levels, and brain function through the production of hormones like thyroxine (T4) and triiodothyronine (T3). When thyroid function is impaired, it can lead to mood disturbances.

1. **Hypothyroidism (Underactive Thyroid) & Depression**

- Low thyroid hormone levels can slow down brain function, leading to fatigue, brain fog, and depressive symptoms.
- Studies suggest that untreated hypothyroidism is associated with an increased risk of major depressive disorder (MDD).

2. **Hyperthyroidism (Overactive Thyroid) & Anxiety**

- Excess thyroid hormones can overstimulate the nervous system, leading to restlessness, irritability, and heightened anxiety.
- Research indicates that hyperthyroidism is significantly linked to anxiety disorders.

3. **Thyroid-Stimulating Hormone (TSH) & Mood Disorders**

- Some studies suggest that abnormal TSH levels may contribute to depression, but findings are mixed.
- Mild thyroid abnormalities may not always cause mood symptoms, but severe imbalances often do.

Managing Thyroid-Related Mood Issues

- Thyroid hormone replacement therapy (for hypothyroidism) can improve depressive symptoms.
- Lifestyle changes like stress management, diet, and exercise can support thyroid health.
- Regular thyroid function tests can help monitor hormone levels and prevent mood disturbances.

Hashimoto's Thyroiditis:

This is not from the thyroid; it is an immune system error that affects the liver, pancreas, and cerebellum as well. Standard dosing with T4 does nothing to fix it!

Vitamins & Minerals (Support thyroid function)

- Selenium: 200 mcg per day – Helps reduce thyroid antibodies.

- Zinc: 10–30 mg per day – Supports immune function and thyroid hormone production.

- Vitamin D: 1,000–4,000 IU per day – Deficiency is linked to autoimmune conditions.

- Magnesium: 200–400 mg per day – Supports metabolism and reduces inflammation.

- Iron: 8–18 mg per day – Important for thyroid hormone synthesis.

Adaptogenic Herbs (Help regulate stress & immune response)

- Ashwagandha: 300–600 mg per day – Supports thyroid hormone balance.

- Rhodiola Rosea: 200–600 mg per day – Helps with fatigue and stress resilience.

- Holy Basil (Tulsi): 300–600 mg per day – Supports immune function and reduces inflammation.

Essential Nutrients (Support thyroid hormone conversion)

- L-Tyrosine: 500–2,000 mg per day – Precursor to thyroid hormones.

- Omega-3 Fatty Acids: 1,000–3,000 mg per day – Reduces inflammation.

- Probiotics: 10–50 billion CFU per day – Supports gut health, which is linked to autoimmune conditions.

Dietary Strategies

- Gluten-Free Diet: May help reduce inflammation and autoimmune response.

- Anti-Inflammatory Diet: Includes nutrient-dense foods like leafy greens, healthy fats, and lean proteins.

- Check Epstein-Barr IgG levels.

ADD (Attention Deficit Disorder) & ADHD (Attention Deficit Hyperactivity Disorder)

While both conditions share similarities, ADHD includes hyperactivity, whereas ADD primarily involves inattention. Some treatments may be more effective for one than the other.

ADHD is strongly linked to dopamine dysfunction. Dopamine is a neurotransmitter that plays a key role in motivation, attention, and reward processing. Research suggests that people with ADHD tend to have lower dopamine levels or dysregulated dopamine transmission, which can contribute to symptoms like impulsivity, difficulty focusing, and hyperactivity.

ADHD medications, such as stimulants like Adderall and Ritalin, work by increasing dopamine levels in the brain to improve focus and impulse control. Brain imaging studies have also shown differences in dopamine-related brain regions in individuals with ADHD.

Some ways to naturally support dopamine levels for ADHD care:

Lifestyle Approaches

- Exercise regularly – Aerobic activities like jogging or swimming can boost dopamine production.

- Eat dopamine-boosting foods – Include protein-rich foods like eggs, fish, lean meats, and nuts.

- Get enough sleep – Poor sleep disrupts dopamine regulation.

- Sunlight exposure – Sunlight stimulates dopamine receptors and mood stability.

- Practice mindfulness – Meditation and relaxation exercises help regulate brain function.

Supplements & Nutrients

- L-Tyrosine – A precursor to dopamine, found in protein-rich foods or supplements.

- Omega-3 Fatty Acids – Found in fish oil; they support brain health.

- Magnesium & Zinc – Vital for neurotransmitter balance.

- Rhodiola Rosea & Mucuna Pruriens – Herbal supplements known to support dopamine production.

Behavioral Strategies

- Dopamine-friendly rewards – Setting small, rewarding goals can encourage dopamine release.

- Creative activities – Art, music, and problem-solving tasks can help stimulate dopamine pathways.

Natural Supplements & Dosages
For Focus & Attention (ADD & ADHD)

- **Omega-3 Fatty Acids:** 1,000–3,000 mg per day – Supports brain function and neurotransmitter balance.

- **Zinc:** 10–30 mg per day – Helps regulate dopamine, which is crucial for focus.

- **Iron:** 8–18 mg per day – Deficiency is linked to attention issues.

- **Magnesium:** 200–400 mg per day – Helps with relaxation and cognitive function.

- **L-Tyrosine:** 500–2,000 mg per day – Supports dopamine production for focus.

For Hyperactivity & Impulsivity (ADHD)

- **L-Theanine:** 100–400 mg per day – Promotes calmness and reduces hyperactivity.

- **GABA:** 250–750 mg per day – Helps regulate excitatory brain activity.

- **Rhodiola Rosea:** 200–600 mg per day – Supports stress resilience and focus.

- **Ashwagandha:** 300–600 mg per day – Helps regulate cortisol and reduce impulsivity.

Dietary & Lifestyle Strategies

- **High-Protein Diet:** Supports neurotransmitter production.

- **Elimination Diet:** Avoid artificial additives, refined sugars, and allergens.

- **Mindfulness & Exercise:** Helps regulate dopamine and improve focus.

INSOMNIA

The connection between pregnenolone and sleep quality is rooted in its influence on the body's hormonal balance. As we age, the natural production of pregnenolone tends to decline, potentially contributing to sleep disturbances and other age-related issues. 5-HTP, a precursor to serotonin, is sometimes used in conjunction with pregnenolone to promote relaxation and improve sleep. Pregnenolone may play a role in circadian rhythm regulation and insomnia relief, primarily through its influence on neurosteroids and hormonal balance.

How Pregnenolone Affects Sleep & Circadian Rhythm

- Supports GABA activity – Pregnenolone converts into allopregnanolone, which enhances GABA, a neurotransmitter that promotes relaxation and sleep.

- **Influences deep sleep** – Some studies suggest pregnenolone may increase slow-wave sleep, the most restorative stage of non-REM sleep.

- **Follows a circadian rhythm** – Pregnenolone levels are highest in the morning and lowest at night, suggesting it may be best taken in the morning.

- **Interacts with other hormones** – It serves as a precursor to progesterone, DHEA, and cortisol, all of which impact sleep cycles.

Dosage & Timing

- Low doses (5–10 mg) may help with relaxation and sleep.

- Higher doses (200 mg+) could lead to insomnia or overstimulation, depending on individual sensitivity.

- Morning dosing aligns with natural hormone rhythms and may prevent sleep disturbances.

- Take it in the morning, when levels are supposed to be the highest.

The sleep cycle progresses through different stages, each characterized by distinct brain wave activity:

1. **Stage 1 (Light Sleep - Theta Waves)**

   - This is the transition from wakefulness to sleep.

   - Brain waves slow down, shifting from alpha (relaxed wakefulness) to theta waves.

   - You may experience brief muscle twitches or a sensation of falling.

2. **Stage 2 (Deeper Light Sleep - Theta Waves)**

   - Theta waves continue, but sleep spindles (bursts of brain activity) and K-complexes (sharp waveforms) appear.

   - The body temperature drops, and heart rate slows.

3. **Stage 3 (Deep Sleep - Delta Waves)**

   - This is the most restorative sleep stage, dominated by slow delta waves.

   - The body repairs tissues, strengthens the immune system, and consolidates memories.

   - Waking up from this stage can cause grogginess.

4. **REM Sleep (Dreaming - Mixed Waves, Including Theta)**

   - Brain activity resembles wakefulness, with theta waves and bursts of beta waves.

   - Dreams occur, and the body experiences temporary paralysis to prevent acting out dreams.

- REM sleep is crucial for emotional processing and cognitive function.

The cycle repeats multiple times throughout the night, with REM sleep becoming longer in later cycles. Each stage plays a vital role in maintaining physical and mental health.

Delta waves are the slowest brain waves (0.5–4 Hz) and are associated with deep sleep and healing. They occur during Stage 3 of non-REM sleep, also known as slow-wave sleep, which is crucial for memory consolidation, immune function, and physical recovery.

Benefits of Delta Waves in Deep Sleep

- **Restorative Healing:** Supports cell repair and immune function.

- **Memory Processing:** Helps consolidate long-term memories.

- **Brain Detoxification:** Aids in clearing metabolic waste, potentially reducing the risk of neurodegenerative diseases.

- **Emotional Regulation:** Deep sleep with delta waves may improve mood stability and stress resilience.

How to Enhance Delta Wave Sleep

- **Reduce Blue Light Exposure:** Avoid screens before bedtime.

- **Magnesium & Melatonin:** Supplements may support deep sleep.

- **Meditation & Binaural Beats:** Listening to delta wave frequencies may promote relaxation.

- **Consistent Sleep Schedule:** Helps regulate circadian rhythms for better deep sleep.

Additionally, blue light blocking glasses are designed to reduce exposure to blue light from screens, which may help with eye strain, headaches, and sleep disturbances.

Popular Blue Light Glasses

- Swanwick Day & Night Orange Glasses – Designed for sleep support.
- Gunnar Anti-Blue-Light Glasses – Popular among gamers.
- VJK Premium Blue Light Blocking Glasses – Affordable option.
- Benicci Blue Light Blocking Glasses – Stylish and effective.
- Livho High Tech Blue Light Glasses – Advanced 99% blue light blocking.
- Brigtlaiff Round Blue Light Blocking Glasses – Classic design.
- GLEASANNA 99.9% Blue Light Blocking Glasses – High protection level.

YouTube has many great subliminals to listen to at night that are eight hours long. The best have delta waves in the background.

Alcohol affects delta wave activity in sleep. Initially, it increases slow-wave sleep (which includes delta waves), making the first half of the night feel deep and restful. However, as the alcohol is metabolized, sleep becomes more fragmented, and alpha wave activity (associated with wakefulness) starts to mix with delta waves, disrupting the restorative effects of sleep. This can lead to frequent awakenings and poorer sleep quality overall.

- So while alcohol might help you fall asleep faster, it can ultimately interfere with deep sleep and leave you feeling less refreshed in the morning.

CBD for Anxiety, Depression, and Sleep:

- **Anxiety & Depression:** A study published in Frontiers in Psychiatry found that medicinal cannabis use was associated with lower self-reported depression and improved sleep quality. Another systematic review in the Journal of Cannabis Research suggested that CBD may help alleviate symptoms of social anxiety disorder and schizophrenia, with moderate evidence supporting its use.

- **Sleep:** A large case series published in The Permanente Journal examined CBD's effects on sleep and anxiety. It found that anxiety scores improved in nearly 80% of participants within the first month, while sleep scores improved in about 67% of cases, though they fluctuated over time.

Boosting GABA (gamma-aminobutyric acid) naturally can help with relaxation, stress reduction, and improved sleep. We will investigate this later in the book.

Chronic Epstein-Barr Virus (EBV)

Chronic Epstein-Barr Virus (EBV) has been linked to anxiety and depression, particularly in cases where the virus remains active or triggers an immune response. In my practice, I find many more patients with EBV correlating with more problems than the medical community will admit. Approximately 90% of adults in the U.S. have Epstein-Barr Virus (EBV) IgG antibodies, indicating past or current infection.

How EBV May Influence Anxiety & Depression

1. **Inflammation & Immune Dysregulation**

   - EBV can cause chronic inflammation, which has been associated with mood disorders.

   - Persistent immune activation may lead to fatigue, brain fog, and depressive symptoms.

2. **Neurotransmitter Disruption**

   - EBV may affect serotonin and dopamine levels, contributing to mood instability.

   - Some studies suggest that viral infections can alter neurotransmitter pathways, increasing susceptibility to anxiety.

3. **Autoimmune & Neurological Effects**

   - EBV has been linked to autoimmune conditions, which can impact brain function and emotional health.

   - Chronic EBV infection may contribute to neuroinflammation, affecting cognitive function and mood.

Managing EBV-Related Mood Symptoms

- Anti-inflammatory diet (rich in antioxidants and omega-3s).

- Immune-supporting supplements (such as vitamin D, zinc, and probiotics).

- Stress management techniques (meditation, exercise, and sleep optimization).

Natural Recommendations That May Help Manage Chronic EBV and Its Links to Anxiety and Depression:

Immune-Supporting Nutrients

- **Vitamin C:** 500–2,000 mg per day – Supports immune function and reduces inflammation.

- **Zinc:** 10–30 mg per day – Helps fight viral infections and supports brain health.

- **Vitamin D:** 1,000–4,000 IU per day – Deficiency is linked to mood disorders and immune dysfunction.

- **Selenium:** 200 mcg per day – May help reduce EBV viral load.

Antiviral & Anti-Inflammatory Herbs

- **Astragalus:** 500–1,500 mg per day – Supports immune resilience.

- **Elderberry:** 300–600 mg per day – Has antiviral properties.

- **Licorice Root:** 400–1,200 mg per day – May help suppress EBV activity.

- **Curcumin (Turmeric):** 500–1,500 mg per day – Reduces inflammation and supports brain health.

- **Lemon Balm Extract** has antiviral properties and may help support the immune system against Epstein-Barr Virus (EBV). It can be obtained from:

- Tea: 1–3 grams of dried lemon balm steeped in hot water.

- Capsules: 300–600 mg per day.

- Tincture: 2–4 mL, taken up to three times daily.

- Essential Oil: Used for aromatherapy, but not typically ingested.

Gut & Brain Health Support

- **Probiotics:** 10–50 billion CFU per day – Supports gut health, which is linked to mood regulation.

- **Omega-3 Fatty Acids:** 1,000–3,000 mg per day – Helps reduce inflammation and support brain function.

- **L-Theanine:** 100–400 mg per day – Promotes relaxation and reduces anxiety.

Lifestyle Strategies

- **Anti-inflammatory diet:** Focus on whole foods, healthy fats, and antioxidant-rich fruits and vegetables.

- **Stress management:** Meditation, yoga, and deep breathing exercises can help regulate the immune system.

- **Adequate sleep:** Poor sleep can worsen EBV symptoms and mood disorders.

Yes, **lemon balm** (Melissa officinalis) has antiviral properties and may help inhibit Epstein-Barr Virus (EBV) activity. Some research suggests that lemon balm can support the immune system and reduce viral replication, making it a potential natural remedy for managing EBV.

Regarding EBV classification, Epstein-Barr Virus has two major types: **Type 1 (T1)** and **Type 2 (T2)**. Both types can infect humans, but T1 EBV is more commonly associated with diseases like infectious mononucleosis and certain cancers, while T2 EBV is less prevalent and may have different effects on immune response.

Alzheimer's Disease:

Inflammation plays a significant role here. Researchers have found that excessive activation of the brain's immune cells—microglia—can drive the progression of the disease. These immune cells, when overactive, contribute to the formation of tau protein tangles, which are a hallmark of Alzheimer's.

Additionally, studies suggest that an immune molecule called STING may be involved in the development of harmful plaques and protein tangles in the brain. Blocking this molecule has shown protective effects in lab mice, indicating a potential avenue for treatment. The interaction between genetic factors and inflammation is also crucial. Different versions of the APOE protein affect how microglia respond to Alzheimer's pathology. APOE4, for example, is linked to increased inflammation and a higher risk of developing the disease, while APOE2 appears to have protective effects.

This growing body of research suggests that targeting inflammation could be a promising strategy for preventing or slowing Alzheimer's progression. Would you like to explore potential anti-inflammatory interventions for brain health?

Several natural products can help reduce brain inflammation and support cognitive health. Here are some key options:

- **Omega-3 fatty acids** – Found in oily fish like salmon, these essential fats help regulate inflammation and support brain function.

- **Chia seeds** – A plant-based source of omega-3s that can be easily added to smoothies or cereals.

- **Turmeric (Curcumin)** – A powerful anti-inflammatory spice that has been linked to improved brain health.

- **Green tea** – Contains antioxidants that help protect the brain from oxidative stress and inflammation.

- **Leafy greens** – Vegetables like spinach and kale are rich in vitamins and minerals that support brain function.

- **Probiotics** – A healthy gut microbiome plays a role in reducing neuroinflammation, making probiotic-rich foods beneficial.

The chemical to help memory is called **Acetylcholine**.

Acetylcholine is a key neurotransmitter involved in memory, learning, and muscle function. While you can't directly supplement acetylcholine, you can support its production by consuming choline-rich foods and certain supplements.

Natural Sources of Choline (Acetylcholine Precursor):

- **Eggs** – One of the best sources of choline, essential for acetylcholine synthesis.

- **Beef liver** – Extremely rich in choline, supporting brain function.

- **Fish (salmon, cod, tuna)** – Provides choline along with omega-3s for brain health.

- **Soybeans** – A plant-based source of choline.

- **Cruciferous vegetables (broccoli, Brussels sprouts)** – Contain moderate amounts of choline.

Vitamin & Supplement Sources:

- **Alpha-GPC** – A highly bioavailable choline supplement that directly supports acetylcholine production.

- **Citicoline** – Another effective choline supplement that enhances cognitive function.

- **Phosphatidylcholine** – Found in lecithin supplements, supporting brain health.

- **Acetyl-L-Carnitine** – Helps maintain acetylcholine levels and supports energy metabolism.

While direct acetylcholine supplements don't exist, some compounds like choline and herbal supplements like Bacopa monnieri, Ginkgo biloba, and Huperzine A can indirectly increase acetylcholine levels.

Parkinson's Disease:

Inflammation is increasingly recognized as a key factor. Chronic neuroinflammation can contribute to the degeneration of dopamine-producing neurons, worsening symptoms like tremors, stiffness, and cognitive decline.

Natural Ways to Reduce Inflammation in Parkinson's:
Here are some approaches that may help:

- **Anti-inflammatory diet** – Eating foods rich in antioxidants and omega-3s can help combat inflammation. This includes berries, turmeric, green tea, and fatty fish.

- **Exercise** – Regular movement, such as yoga, tai chi, or walking, can reduce inflammation and improve motor function.

- **Supplements** – Some studies suggest that Coenzyme Q10 (CoQ10), NADH, and green tea extract may offer neuroprotective benefits.

- **Herbal remedies** – Certain herbs, like ashwagandha and ginkgo biloba, have been explored for their potential to support brain health.

- **Gut health** – Maintaining a healthy gut microbiome with probiotics and fiber-rich foods may help regulate inflammation.

- **Antioxidant-rich diet** – Foods like berries, dark chocolate, green tea, and nuts help combat oxidative stress.

Grief:

Losing a loved one profoundly impacts the brain, triggering a cascade of chemical changes. Grief increases cortisol, the stress hormone, which can overwhelm the prefrontal cortex, leading to mental fog and difficulty concentrating. The amygdala, responsible for emotional processing, becomes hyperactive, intensifying feelings of fear, sadness, and anxiety.

At the same time, levels of serotonin and dopamine—key neurotransmitters for mood regulation and reward—tend to drop, contributing to prolonged sadness, low energy, and even physical fatigue. Grief also disrupts brainwave patterns, reducing alpha waves (linked to relaxation) and increasing theta waves, which are associated with deep emotional processing.

The brain interprets grief as emotional trauma, engaging the fight-or-flight response, which releases stress hormones and affects memory, sleep, and cognitive function. Over time, chronic grief can rewire neural pathways, reinforcing emotional distress and making it harder to move forward.

Several herbs, vitamins, and natural supplements can help support brain health and emotional resilience during grief:

Herbs for Grief Support:

- **Lavender** – Calms the nervous system, eases anxiety, and promotes restful sleep.

- **Chamomile** – Helps reduce stress and tension, supports digestion, and encourages relaxation.

- **Hawthorn** – A heart tonic that supports emotional healing and cardiovascular health.

- **Rose** – Known for its gentle antidepressant properties, it uplifts emotions and promotes self-love.

Vitamins & Nutrients for Brain Health:

- **Magnesium** – Helps regulate the stress response and supports cognitive function.

- **Omega-3 Fatty Acids** – Found in fish oil, these support mood stability and brain health.

- **Vitamin D** – Plays a role in mood regulation and emotional well-being.

- **B Vitamins** – Essential for neurotransmitter function and energy production.

These natural remedies can complement other healing strategies like therapy, mindfulness, and physical activity.

YouTube videos with alpha and theta beats can also be helpful.

Addiction Behaviors and Support Recovery:

1. **Herbal Remedies**

   Certain herbs are believed to help with withdrawal symptoms and cravings:

   - **Milk Thistle** – Supports liver detoxification, especially for alcohol addiction.

   - **Ashwagandha** – Helps reduce stress and anxiety, which can trigger addictive behaviors.

   - **Passionflower** – Used for calming the nervous system and reducing withdrawal symptoms.

   - **Kudzu Root** – May help reduce alcohol cravings.

   - **Rhodiola Rosea** – Supports mood balance and energy levels during recovery.

2. **Nutritional Supplements**

   Deficiencies in vitamins and minerals can contribute to addictive cravings:

   - **Omega-3 Fatty Acids** – Support brain health and emotional stability.

   - **Magnesium** – Helps with relaxation and stress reduction.

   - **Vitamin B Complex** – Supports nervous system function and energy levels.

   - **L-Tyrosine** – May help restore dopamine levels affected by addiction.

- **N-Acetyl Cysteine (NAC)** – Has been studied for reducing cravings in substance use disorders.

3. **Mindfulness & Meditation**

   Practices like meditation, deep breathing, and yoga can help manage stress and emotional triggers that lead to addiction.

4. **Acupuncture**

   Certain acupuncture points may help reduce cravings and withdrawal symptoms. Ear acupuncture, in particular, is used in addiction recovery programs.

5. **Exercise & Physical Activity**

   Regular exercise helps regulate dopamine levels and reduces stress, which can lower the risk of relapse.

6. **Aromatherapy**

   Essential oils like lavender, peppermint, and bergamot may help with relaxation and emotional balance.

Diets and the Environment:

Each of these diets—Carnivore, Keto, and Mediterranean—affects mental health differently due to their impact on inflammation, neurotransmitter balance, and gut health.

Carnivore Diet & Mental Health

- **Potential Benefits:** Some people report improved mental clarity, reduced anxiety, and stabilized mood due to the elimination of processed foods and carbohydrates.

- **Concerns:** Lack of fiber and plant-based nutrients may affect gut microbiome diversity, which plays a role in mood regulation.

Keto Diet & Mental Health

- Potential Benefits: Keto promotes ketone production, which may enhance brain function and reduce symptoms of depression and anxiety.

- **Concerns:** Some individuals experience "keto flu," which can temporarily cause brain fog and mood swings.

Mediterranean Diet & Mental Health

- **Potential Benefits:** Rich in omega-3s, fiber, and antioxidants, this diet is linked to lower rates of depression and cognitive decline.

- **Concerns:** While generally beneficial, excessive carbohydrate intake from grains may contribute to blood sugar fluctuations, affecting mood.

Possible Links Between Monsanto Products & Mental Health

There is ongoing debate about the potential health effects of Monsanto products, particularly those containing glyphosate (the active ingredient in Roundup) and genetically modified organisms (GMOs). While there is no direct evidence proving that Monsanto products cause anxiety or depression, some studies suggest that ultra-processed foods—which may contain ingredients from genetically modified crops—could be linked to mental health issues.

1. **Ultra-Processed Foods & Depression**

   - Research suggests that diets high in ultra-processed foods may increase the risk of depression and anxiety.

   - These foods often contain artificial additives, preservatives, and refined sugars, which may disrupt gut health and neurotransmitter balance.

2. **Glyphosate & Gut-Brain Axis**

   - Some studies indicate that glyphosate exposure may affect the gut microbiome, which plays a role in mental health.

   - Disruptions in gut bacteria have been linked to mood disorders, but more research is needed to confirm glyphosate's direct impact.

3. **Inflammation & Mental Health**

- Certain food additives and pesticides may contribute to chronic inflammation, which has been associated with depression and anxiety.

What Can You Do?

- Focus on whole, minimally processed foods to support brain health.

- Choose organic produce if you're concerned about pesticide exposure.

- Monitor your diet and see if certain foods affect your mood.

Hormones Linked to Anxiety & Depression

Hormones play a significant role in anxiety and depression, as they regulate mood, stress response, and brain function. Imbalances in certain hormones can contribute to mental health challenges:

1. **Cortisol (Stress Hormone)**

- Elevated cortisol levels due to chronic stress can lead to anxiety, irritability, and sleep disturbances.

- Low cortisol levels may contribute to fatigue and depression.

2. **Thyroid Hormones (T3 & T4)**

- Hypothyroidism (low thyroid function) is linked to depression, brain fog, and fatigue.

- Hyperthyroidism (overactive thyroid) can cause anxiety, restlessness, and mood swings.

3. **Serotonin & Dopamine (Neurotransmitters)**

- Serotonin helps regulate mood, and low levels are associated with depression and anxiety.

- Dopamine influences motivation and pleasure, and imbalances can lead to low energy and mood instability.

4. **Estrogen & Progesterone (Sex Hormones)**

   - Fluctuations in estrogen can impact serotonin levels, affecting mood.

   - Low progesterone may contribute to anxiety and sleep disturbances.

5. **Testosterone**

   - Low testosterone levels in both men and women can lead to depression, fatigue, and irritability.

Managing Hormonal Imbalances for Mental Health

- Lifestyle changes: Regular exercise, stress management, and a balanced diet can help regulate hormones.

- Supplements: Nutrients like magnesium, vitamin D, and omega-3s support hormone balance.

- Medical evaluation: If symptoms persist, hormone testing may help identify imbalances.

The Brain-Gut Axis refers to the complex communication network that links the central nervous system (CNS) and the enteric nervous system (ENS) of the gastrointestinal tract. This bidirectional communication involves neural, hormonal, and immunological signaling pathways. This supports mental well-being by maintaining microbial balance, neurotransmitter production, and immune function:

- Depressed and anxious guts often show inflammation, microbial imbalances, and neurotransmitter disruptions.

- Improving gut health through diet, probiotics, and stress management may help alleviate symptoms.

1. **Central Nervous System (CNS):** The brain and spinal cord, which process and integrate information.

2. **Enteric Nervous System (ENS):** Often referred to as the "second brain," it consists of a network of neurons embedded in the walls of the gastrointestinal tract.

3. **Vagus Nerve:** A major nerve that transmits signals between the brain and the gut.

4. **Gut Microbiota:** The diverse community of microorganisms in the gut that influence and are influenced by the brain.

5. **Neurotransmitters and Hormones:** Chemical messengers like serotonin, dopamine, and cortisol that facilitate communication between the brain and gut. The exact number of neurotransmitters in humans is unknown, but more than 100 have been identified. We will talk about the most common ones in this book.

The 4R Protocol

The 4R Protocol is a well-known approach to gut healing, focusing on restoring digestive health. Here's how it works:

1. **Remove** – Eliminate harmful substances like processed foods, toxins, infections, and inflammatory triggers that contribute to gut dysfunction.

2. **Replace** – Support digestion by adding essential nutrients, digestive enzymes, and stomach acid to improve nutrient absorption.

3. **Reinoculate** – Restore beneficial gut bacteria with probiotics and prebiotics to balance the microbiome.

4. **Repair** – Strengthen the gut lining with nutrients like glutamine, zinc, and omega-3s to reduce inflammation and improve intestinal integrity.

This method is commonly used to address leaky gut, IBS, and other digestive disorders.

Here's how you can support each step of the 4R gut repair protocol with foods and supplements:

1. **Remove (Eliminate Harmful Triggers)**

   - Avoid processed foods, sugar, alcohol, and inflammatory foods.

   - Consider antimicrobial herbs like garlic, oregano oil, and berberine to help remove harmful bacteria.

   - Support detoxification with fiber-rich foods like flaxseeds, chia seeds, and leafy greens.

2. **Replace (Support Digestion)**

- Digestive enzymes (bromelain, papain) help break down food efficiently.

- Betaine HCl supports stomach acid production for better digestion.

- Ginger & peppermint aid digestion and reduce bloating.

3. **Reinoculate (Restore Gut Bacteria)**

- Probiotic-rich foods: Yogurt, kefir, sauerkraut, kimchi, and miso.

- Prebiotic foods: Bananas, onions, garlic, asparagus, and oats.

- Probiotic supplements: Look for strains like Lactobacillus and Bifidobacterium.

4. **Repair (Heal the Gut Lining)**

- L-glutamine: Supports intestinal lining repair.

- Zinc & omega-3s: Reduce inflammation and promote healing.

- Bone broth & collagen: Provide amino acids for gut repair.

- Aloe vera & slippery elm: Soothe and protect the gut lining.

The 4R gut repair protocol typically lasts 6 to 8 weeks, but the duration can vary based on individual needs and health conditions. Some people may require a longer period, especially if dealing with chronic gut issues like leaky gut, IBS, or autoimmune conditions.

- Acute gut imbalances: 4–6 weeks may be sufficient.

- Chronic gut issues: 8+ weeks or ongoing maintenance may be needed.

- Severe gut dysbiosis: Some individuals follow a modified version for several months.

The gut microbiome plays a crucial role in mental health, and differences in gut composition can influence mood disorders like depression and anxiety.

Normal Gut

- Balanced microbiome with diverse beneficial bacteria.

- Healthy levels of short-chain fatty acids (SCFAs), which support brain function.

- Strong gut barrier, preventing inflammation and harmful substances from entering the bloodstream.

- Optimal serotonin and dopamine production, contributing to stable mood.

Depressed Gut

- Reduced diversity of gut bacteria, often with lower levels of Firmicutes and Faecalibacterium.

- Increased pro-inflammatory bacteria, leading to chronic inflammation.

- Lower production of SCFAs, which are essential for brain health.

- Possible leaky gut, allowing toxins to enter the bloodstream and affect brain function.

- Disruptions in serotonin metabolism, contributing to low mood.

Anxiety Gut

- Higher levels of stress-related bacteria, such as Enterobacteriaceae and Fusobacterium.

- Reduced GABA-producing bacteria, leading to heightened stress response.

- Increased gut permeability, which may trigger inflammation and nervous system dysregulation.

- Altered gut-brain communication, affecting neurotransmitter balance.

Here are some foods and natural supplements that may help support leaky gut healing, along with typical dosages:

Gut-Healing Foods

- Bone Broth: Rich in collagen and amino acids that support gut lining repair.

- Fermented Foods (Sauerkraut, Kimchi, Kefir): Contain probiotics that help restore gut microbiome balance.

- Omega-3-Rich Foods (Salmon, Chia Seeds, Walnuts): Reduce inflammation and support gut health.

- Prebiotic Fiber (Garlic, Onions, Asparagus): Feeds beneficial gut bacteria, promoting gut barrier integrity.

Natural Supplements & Dosages

- L-Glutamine: 5–10 g per day – Supports gut lining repair and reduces intestinal permeability.

- Probiotics: 10–50 billion CFU per day – Helps restore gut microbiome balance.

- Collagen Peptides: 5–15 g per day – Supports gut lining and connective tissue health.

- Zinc Carnosine: 75–150 mg per day – Helps strengthen gut barrier function.

- Curcumin (Turmeric): 500–1,500 mg per day – Reduces inflammation and supports gut healing.

- Aloe Vera: 50–200 mg per day – Soothes gut lining and supports digestion.

These foods and supplements may help reduce gut inflammation, repair intestinal permeability, and support microbiome balance. Many herbs and nutrients—such as marshmallow, slippery elm, glutamine, and zinc carnosine—have been shown to help heal a leaky gut.

Bloating & Gas

- Probiotics: 10–50 billion CFU per day – Helps restore gut balance and improve digestion.

- Activated Charcoal: 500–1,000 mg per day – Helps absorb excess gas and toxins.

- Ginger: 500–2,000 mg per day – Reduces bloating and improves gut motility.

Food Sensitivities & Allergies

- L-Glutamine: 5–10 g per day – Repairs gut lining and reduces food sensitivity reactions.

- Digestive Enzymes: Take with meals – Supports nutrient absorption and breaks down food efficiently.

- Quercetin: 500–1,500 mg per day – Helps reduce inflammation and histamine reactions.

Brain Fog & Fatigue

- Omega-3 Fatty Acids: 1,000–3,000 mg per day – Supports brain function and reduces inflammation.

- Vitamin B Complex: Dosage varies – Supports energy production and neurotransmitter balance.

- CoQ10: 100–300 mg per day – Helps with cellular energy production.

Constipation & Slow Digestion

- Magnesium Citrate: 200–400 mg per day – Relieves constipation and relaxes intestinal muscles.

- Aloe Vera: 50–200 mg per day – Helps soothe digestion and support gut lining.

- Psyllium Husk: 5–10 g per day – Provides fiber to promote healthy digestion.

Chronic Inflammation & Autoimmune Issues

- Turmeric (Curcumin): 500–1,500 mg per day – Reduces gut inflammation.

- Bone Broth: 1–2 cups per day – Provides collagen and amino acids for gut repair.

- Vitamin D: 1,000–4,000 IU per day – Supports immune function and gut integrity.

These recommendations are tailored to different symptoms, but gut healing is a long-term process that requires consistency.

Does Turmeric Pull Metals from the Liver?

- Turmeric contains curcumin, which has antioxidant and anti-inflammatory properties.

- Some studies suggest that curcumin may help reduce heavy metal toxicity by supporting liver detoxification.

- However, turmeric does not directly "pull" metals from the liver—it may support liver function and reduce oxidative stress caused by heavy metals.

Does Turmeric Cause Anemia?

- Some research indicates that turmeric may inhibit iron absorption, potentially contributing to iron deficiency anemia in individuals with low iron levels.

- Turmeric contains polyphenols, which can bind to iron and reduce its bioavailability.

- However, human studies suggest that turmeric supplements do not significantly inhibit iron absorption when consumed in normal dietary amounts.

Short-Chain Fatty Acids (SCFAs)

Short-chain fatty acids (SCFAs) are fatty acids with two to six carbon atoms and play a crucial role in gut health. The main SCFAs include:

- **Acetic acid (C2:0)** – Supports energy metabolism and gut health.

- **Propionic acid (C3:0)** – Helps regulate glucose metabolism and reduces inflammation.

- **Butyric acid (C4:0)** – Essential for colon health and provides energy to gut cells.

- **Isobutyric acid (C4:0)** – A branched SCFA with metabolic benefits.

- **Valeric acid (C5:0)** – May have neuroprotective effects.

- **Isovaleric acid (C5:0)** – Involved in metabolic processes.

SCFAs are primarily produced in the gut through the fermentation of dietary fiber by beneficial bacteria. They contribute to immune function, digestion, and overall metabolic health.

Great choice! Eating fiber-rich foods helps promote short-chain fatty acid (SCFA) production in the gut. Here are some of the best options:

- **Oats** – Rich in beta-glucan, which stimulates butyrate production.

- **Chia & Flaxseeds** – High in soluble fiber, supporting SCFA formation.

- **Legumes (lentils, chickpeas, beans)** – Excellent sources of fermentable fiber.

- **Vegetables (broccoli, cabbage, onions)** – Provide fiber that feeds gut bacteria.

- **Fruits (bananas, apples, berries)** – Contain pectin, which enhances SCFA production.

- **Fermented foods (kimchi, yogurt, kefir)** – Support gut microbiome health.

- **Whole grains (brown rice, quinoa, barley)** – Help maintain SCFA balance.

The fermentation of fiber in the gut is primarily carried out by beneficial bacteria, which produce short-chain fatty acids (SCFAs) like butyrate, acetate, and propionate. Some of the key bacterial groups involved include:

- **Bifidobacteria** – Help break down fiber and support gut health.

- **Lactobacilli** – Common in fermented foods; aid digestion and immunity.

- **Firmicutes** (e.g., Faecalibacterium, Clostridium) – Produce butyrate, which nourishes gut cells.

- **Bacteroidetes** – Help metabolize complex carbohydrates and fiber.

- **Akkermansia muciniphila** – Supports gut barrier function and metabolism.

SCFAs are a must in any thriving diet plan. Take this seriously, please!

TESTING:

Measuring brain chemical levels can be tricky because neurotransmitters operate within the brain and are protected by the blood-brain barrier. However, there are several indirect methods used in research and clinical settings:

Methods to Measure Brain Chemicals

1. **Urine Tests** – Some neurotransmitters and their metabolites are excreted in urine, allowing for indirect measurement of levels like dopamine, serotonin, and GABA.

2. **Blood Tests** – While neurotransmitters are present in the bloodstream, their levels may not accurately reflect brain activity due to the blood-brain barrier.

3. **Saliva Tests** – Certain hormones and neurotransmitter-related compounds can be detected in saliva, though this method is less common.

4. **Magnetic Resonance Spectroscopy (MRS)** – A non-invasive imaging technique similar to MRI that can measure brain metabolites and neurotransmitter activity.

5. **PET Scans** – Positron Emission Tomography can track neurotransmitter activity by using specialized tracers, often used in research on dopamine and serotonin.

The DUTCH test, which stands for **Dried Urine Test for Comprehensive Hormones**, is a valuable tool in examining mental health conditions. This test measures a wide range of hormones and their metabolites from dried urine samples, providing insights into various physiological and pathological conditions.

One of the key aspects of the DUTCH test is its ability to measure cortisol levels and patterns throughout the day. Cortisol is a hormone produced by the adrenal glands and plays a crucial role in the body's response to stress. By analyzing cortisol levels, the DUTCH test can help identify conditions related to chronic stress and fatigue, such as hypothalamic-pituitary-adrenal (HPA) axis dysfunction and immune dysregulation.

The test also evaluates the balance of neurotransmitters through methylation processes, which involve the transfer of methyl groups to and from molecules. Imbalances in methylation can lead to altered levels of neurotransmitters, resulting in cognitive and emotional disturbances.

The DUTCH test measures neurotransmitter metabolites in urine, providing insights into GABA, dopamine, serotonin, and epinephrine levels. Here are the key markers:

- **Homovanillate (HVA)** – A dopamine metabolite; low levels may indicate dopamine deficiency, leading to fatigue, low motivation, and depression.

- **Vanilmandelate (VMA)** – A metabolite of epinephrine and norepinephrine; low levels suggest reduced adrenal function and possible neurotransmitter imbalance.

- **5-Hydroxyindoleacetate (5-HIAA)** – A serotonin metabolite; low levels may indicate serotonin deficiency, contributing to mood disorders and sleep disturbances.

- **Serotonin (5-HT)** is primarily broken down by the enzyme monoamine oxidase (MAO) into 5-hydroxyindoleacetic acid (5-HIAA), which is then excreted in urine.

- **Norepinephrine** is metabolized by MAO and catechol-O-methyltransferase (COMT) into vanillylmandelic acid (VMA), which is also eliminated from the body.

Hydroxytryptamine (5-HT, also known as serotonin) and **norepinephrine** undergo metabolic processes in the body:

- **Serotonin (5-HT)** is primarily broken down by the enzyme monoamine oxidase (MAO) into 5-hydroxyindoleacetic acid (5-HIAA), which is then excreted in urine.
- **Norepinephrine** is metabolized by MAO and catechol-O-methyltransferase (COMT) into vanillylmandelic acid (VMA), which is also eliminated from the body.

REMEMBER: In teenagers currently in the phase of development and growth, the 5-hydroxytryptamine (5-HT) and norepinephrine neurotransmitter systems in the nervous system are not yet mature. The response to antidepressants is different from that of adults.

Accession # 00280399
Female Sample Report
123 A Street
Sometown , CA 90266

Last Menstrual Period:

Ordering Physician:
Precision Analytical

DOB: 1953-10-10
Age: 63
Gender: Female

Collection Times:
2016-10-02 06:00AM
2016-10-02 06:00AM
2016-10-01 06:00PM
2016-10-01 10:00PM
2016-10-02 02:00AM

Hormone Testing Summary

Sex Hormones See Pages 2 and 3 for a thorough breakdown of sex hormone metabolites

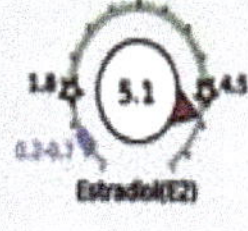

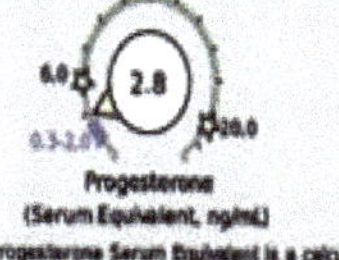

Progesterone Serum Equivalent is a calculated
value based on urine pregnanediol.

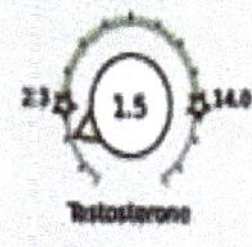

Adrenal Hormones See pages 4 and 5 for a more complete breakdown of adrenal hormones

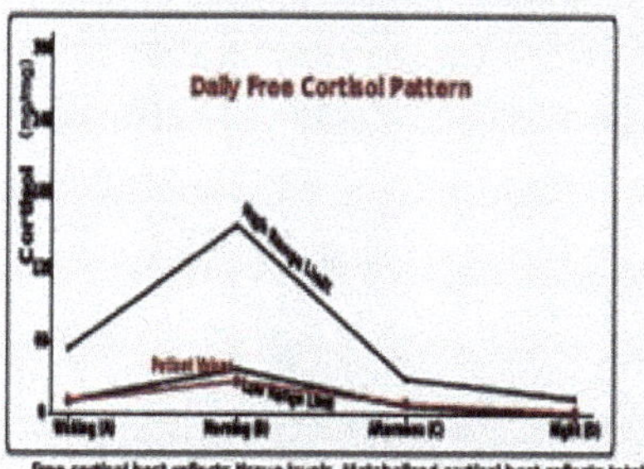

Total DHEA Production

Age	Range
20-39	1300-3000
40-60	750-2000
>60	500-1200

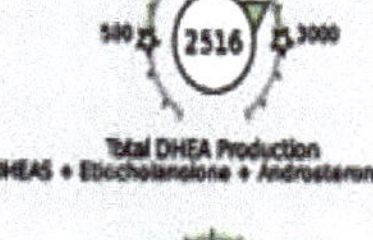

cortisol
metabolism

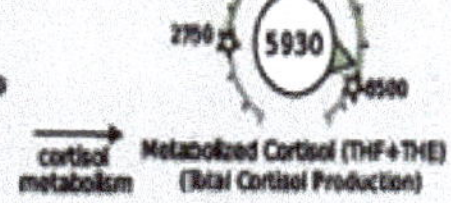

Free cortisol best reflects tissue levels. Metabolized cortisol best reflects total cortisol production.

The following videos (which can also be found on the website under the listed names along with others) may aid your understanding:
DUTCH Complete Overview   Estrogen Tutorial   Female Androgen Tutorial   Cortisol Tutorial

PLEASE BE SURE TO READ BELOW FOR ANY SPECIFIC LAB COMMENTS. More detailed comments can be found on page 8.

The **Neurolab-Sanesco neurotransmitter test** is also a valuable tool for assessing mental health conditions by measuring the levels of various neurotransmitters and adrenal hormones. Neurotransmitters are chemical messengers in the brain that play a crucial role in regulating mood, cognition, and overall mental health. Imbalances in these neurotransmitters can lead to various mental health issues such as anxiety, depression, insomnia, and fatigue.

The Sanesco test focuses on the **hypothalamic-pituitary-adrenal (HPA) axis**, which is essential for the body's stress response and overall neuroendocrine function. By analyzing neurotransmitters like **serotonin, GABA, glutamate, dopamine, norepinephrine, and epinephrine**, the test can identify imbalances that may be contributing to mental health symptoms.

Additionally, the test includes assessments of **adrenal hormones** like **cortisol** and **DHEA-S**, which are important for managing stress and energy levels. The results of the test can help healthcare providers develop personalized treatment plans that address the specific imbalances and improve mental health outcomes.

No guesswork here. The major brain chemicals and cortisol levels are clearly defined in the report.

The foremost reference laboratory for the measurement of biomarkers associated with HPA-T axis function.

HPA Profile (1) (Hypothalamic-Pituitary-Adrenal Axis)

Anita Doc
ID#: 301458
Gender: F   Age: 51

Will Fiksu, MD
123 Serotonin Pathway
Sanesco, NC 00001

Date Reported
09/07/2015

Date Collected
08/23/2015

Date Received
08/29/2015

Lab Final
09/03/2015

Report Final
09/07/2015

Marker	Values		Optimal	Reference
INHIBITORY NEUROTRANSMITTERS				
SEROTONIN	42.5	(L)	125 - 260 mcg/g Cr	50-250 mcg/g Cr
GABA	137.2	(L)	600 - 1100 mcg/g Cr	150-700 mcg/g Cr
EXCITATORY NEUROTRANSMITTERS				
DOPAMINE	104.7	(L)	250 - 400 mcg/g Cr	100-350 mcg/g Cr
NOR-EPINEPHRINE	27.0	(L)	30 - 50 mcg/g Cr	13-70 mcg/g Cr
EPINEPHRINE	4.1	(L)	10 - 15 mcg/g Cr	3-20 mcg/g Cr
GLUTAMATE	20.3	(H)	5 - 10 mg/g Cr	2-12 mg/g Cr
ADRENAL ADAPTATION INDEX				
NOREPI/EPI RATIO	6.6		n/a	<13
ADRENAL HORMONES				
CORTISOL (0830)	4.9	(L)	n/a	5.1-11.6 nM
CORTISOL (1245)	2.0	(L)	n/a	2.3-5.3 nM
CORTISOL (1700)	1.1		n/a	1.0-2.4 nM
CORTISOL (2130)	0.2	(L)	n/a	.4-2.1 nM
DHEA-s (0830)	1.1		n/a	1.0-3.0 ng/ml
DHEA-s (1700)	1.4		n/a	1.0-3.0 ng/ml
OTHER MARKERS				
CREATININE, URINE	100.0		n/a	mg/dL

Creatinine is used to calculate results and is not intended to be used diagnostically.
(L) & (H) are based on optimal range intervals.

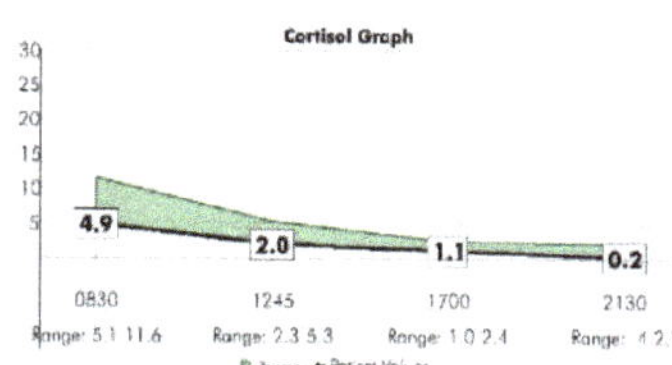

Results Processed By COLA # 24550, NeuroLab Asheville, NC

Modern Allergy Management tests can help identify potential mental health issues by examining the body's reactions to various allergens and intolerances. These tests often use **bioresonance hair testing**, which is a non-invasive method that analyzes the electromagnetic waves generated by particles in the body. This technique can detect sensitivities to over 750 food and non-food items, as well as metals and minerals.

1. By identifying intolerances and sensitivities, the test can help pinpoint triggers that may contribute to mental health symptoms such as anxiety, depression, and cognitive disturbances. For example, certain food intolerances or heavy metal exposures can exacerbate symptoms of ADHD or other mental health conditions.

2. Understanding these triggers allows individuals to make dietary and lifestyle changes that can improve their overall mental well-being.

3. Allergic responses can influence mental health, potentially contributing to anxiety, depression, and even schizophrenia-like symptoms. Research suggests that allergies trigger chronic inflammation, which can affect brain function and mood. Here's how:

   - **Inflammation & Neurotransmitters:** Allergic reactions increase cytokines, which can disrupt serotonin and dopamine levels, leading to mood disturbances.

   - **Histamine & Anxiety:** High histamine levels, common in allergies, have been linked to heightened anxiety and irritability.

   - **Sleep Disruptions:** Allergies can interfere with sleep, worsening symptoms of depression and cognitive function.

- **Schizophrenia Connection:** Some studies suggest a correlation between seasonal allergies and schizophrenia, though the relationship is complex and not fully understood.

While allergies don't directly cause mental illness, they can exacerbate symptoms in susceptible individuals.

If you need help getting these tests, just email me at john@ask-drjohn.com, and we'll set you up.

Genova Diagnostics is the grandfather of the stool test and still my favorite:

The health of the entire body is dependent on a healthy gut and gut microbiome. Gut microbes are codependent with one another and with their human host, and the health of one affects the other. A sizeable volume of research associates a dysbiotic, or imbalanced, gut microbiome with multiple disease states both within and outside of the GI tract, including moods and brain transmitters. The diverse metabolic activities of the microbiome ultimately impact the human host, and the activities of the human host ultimately affect the health of their microbiome.

The **GI Effects Stool Profiles** are a suite of advanced stool tests that provide immediate, actionable clinical information for the management of gastrointestinal health. Utilizing cutting-edge technologies and biomarkers, these profiles offer valuable insight into digestive function, intestinal inflammation, and the intestinal microbiome. The overview pages make results interpretation quicker and easier, to prioritize treatment and assess microbiome status.

3425 Corporate Way
Duluth, GA 30096

Patient: **SAMPLE**
PATIENT
DOB:
Sex:
MRN:

2200 GI Effects™ Comprehensive Profile - Stool

Powered by Genova AI

Results Overview

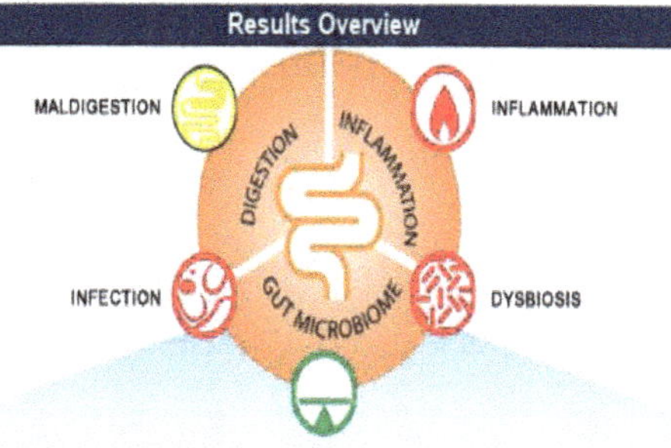

Functional Imbalance Scores

Key (< 2) : Low Need for Support (2-3) : Optional Need for Support (4-6) : Moderate Need for Support (7-10) : High Need for Support

Questionnaires:

Health professionals use structured questions to assess anxiety, PTSD, and depression. Some common questions used in evaluations:

Anxiety

- Do you often feel restless or on edge?
- Do you experience excessive worry that is difficult to control?
- Do you have physical symptoms like rapid heartbeat, sweating, or trembling?
- Do you avoid situations due to fear or nervousness?

PTSD

- Have you experienced a traumatic event that still affects you?
- Do you have flashbacks or nightmares related to the event?
- Do you avoid places, people, or activities that remind you of the trauma?
- Do you feel emotionally numb or disconnected from others?
- Do you startle easily or feel constantly on guard?

Depression

- Have you felt sad or hopeless for most of the day, nearly every day?
- Have you lost interest in activities you once enjoyed?
- Do you experience changes in appetite or sleep patterns?
- Do you feel fatigued or have difficulty concentrating?
- Have you had thoughts of self-harm or suicide?

Bipolar Disorder Questions:

Manic or Hypomanic Episodes

- Have you ever felt unusually energetic or euphoric for extended periods?

- Do you experience racing thoughts or feel like your mind won't slow down?

- Have you engaged in impulsive behaviors, such as excessive spending or risky activities?

- Do you feel like you need little to no sleep but still function well?

Depressive Episodes

- Have you experienced prolonged feelings of sadness or hopelessness?

- Do you struggle with motivation or lose interest in activities you once enjoyed?

- Have you noticed significant changes in appetite or sleep patterns?

- Do you feel fatigued or have difficulty concentrating?

- Have you lost interest in hobbies?

- Do you have unprovoked anger?

Mood Swings & Patterns

- Do you experience extreme shifts in mood that last for days or weeks?

- Have others commented on noticeable changes in your behavior or energy levels?

- Do you feel like your emotions are unpredictable or difficult to control?

GABA Issues

- Do you panic for no reason?

- Do you feel overwhelmed?

- How hard is it to turn off your mind?

- Are you worrying more about things you once controlled?

- Do you feel guilty making decisions?

- Feelings of dread or doom?

- Insomnia?

More on GABA in a couple of pages.

Neurotransmitters Most Tested:

Low Serotonin

Low levels in the colon can affect digestion and gut function in several ways. Since about 95% of the body's serotonin is produced in the gut, it plays a crucial role in regulating bowel movements and intestinal sensitivity. When serotonin levels are low, it can lead to constipation, slower food movement through the intestines, and increased pain sensitivity.

People with irritable bowel syndrome (IBS) who experience constipation often have lower serotonin levels, making their intestines less reactive to serotonin, which can result in harder stools. Additionally, serotonin deficiency in the gut has been linked to heightened pain sensitivity and even conditions like fibromyalgia. Serotonin in the gut is primarily produced by enterochromaffin (EC) cells, which are scattered throughout the small intestine and colon. These cells work alongside gut bacteria to regulate serotonin levels, influencing digestion, gut motility, and even mood.

- Eat tryptophan-rich foods: Tryptophan is an amino acid that helps produce serotonin. Foods like turkey, eggs, salmon, nuts, and seeds are great sources.

- Consume probiotics: A healthy gut microbiome supports serotonin production. Fermented foods like yogurt, kimchi, sauerkraut, and kefir can help.

- Get sunlight: Sun exposure increases serotonin levels, so spending time outdoors can be beneficial.

Low Dopamine

Foods to Support Dopamine Levels

- Protein-rich foods: Turkey, beef, eggs, dairy, and soy contain tyrosine, a precursor to dopamine.

- Probiotic-rich foods: Fermented foods like yogurt, kimchi, sauerkraut, and kefir may support dopamine production.

- Dark chocolate: Contains compounds that may enhance dopamine release.

- Nuts and seeds: Almonds, walnuts, and pumpkin seeds provide nutrients that support brain health.

- Bananas: Rich in L-tyrosine, which helps produce dopamine.

- Green leafy vegetables: Spinach and kale contain folate, which plays a role in dopamine synthesis.

Natural Supplements for Dopamine

- L-Tyrosine: A direct precursor to dopamine; commonly taken in doses of 500–2000 mg per day.

- Mucuna Pruriens: Contains L-DOPA, a dopamine precursor; doses range from 300–500 mg daily.

- Rhodiola Rosea: May help regulate dopamine levels and reduce mental fatigue.

- Vitamin B6, B9, and B12: Support dopamine production and brain function.

- CoQ10 and Acetyl-L-Carnitine: May enhance dopamine-related cognitive functions.

Acetylcholine

Acetylcholine is a neurotransmitter that plays a crucial role in memory, learning, and muscle function. To naturally boost acetylcholine levels, you can incorporate choline-rich foods into your diet. Here are some top sources:

- Egg yolks – One of the best sources of choline

- Liver – Beef and chicken liver are packed with choline

- Salmon – A great source of both choline and omega-3 fatty acids

- Beef – Contains choline along with essential nutrients

- Cauliflower – A plant-based source of choline

- Milk and dairy products – Provide choline and other brain-supporting nutrients

- Quinoa and amaranth – Whole grains that contribute to acetylcholine production

- Edamame and cruciferous vegetables – Help support neurotransmitter function

Symptoms of Low Acetylcholine

- Mental: Memory problems, confusion, difficulty concentrating, depression, disrupted sleep

- Physical: Muscle weakness, fatigue, slower digestion, lower heart rate

Symptoms of High Acetylcholine

- Mental: Anxiety, heightened stress, hallucinations (in extreme cases)

- Physical: Muscle cramps, excessive contractions, digestive overstimulation, rapid heart rate, depressed breathing (in severe cases)

To Boost Acetylcholine

- Eat choline-rich foods: Eggs, liver, salmon, beef, dairy, cauliflower, quinoa, and soy products

- Exercise regularly: Physical activity helps enhance neurotransmitter balance

- Get enough sleep: Proper rest supports acetylcholine production

- Use brain-training exercises: Mental stimulation encourages acetylcholine activity

To Lower Excess Acetylcholine

- Balance your diet: Reduce excessive choline intake from supplements if needed

- Manage stress: Chronic stress can raise acetylcholine levels, so relaxation techniques help

- Consult a doctor: If symptoms persist, professional guidance may be necessary

Acetylcholine Imbalances Can Be Influenced by Various Diseases and Habits. Here's How:

Conditions and Habits That Increase Acetylcholine

- Neurotoxins and poisoning – Exposure to certain toxins or pesticides can lead to excessive acetylcholine

- Chronic stress – Prolonged stress can elevate acetylcholine levels, contributing to anxiety and muscle tension

- Certain medications – Some drugs, like cholinesterase inhibitors used for Alzheimer's, increase acetylcholine

- Excessive choline intake – Overconsumption of choline-rich foods or supplements can lead to high acetylcholine

Conditions and Habits That Decrease Acetylcholine

- Neurodegenerative diseases – Alzheimer's, Parkinson's, and Multiple Sclerosis are linked to low acetylcholine

- Poor diet – A diet lacking in choline-rich foods (like eggs, liver, and salmon) can reduce acetylcholine

- Chronic inflammation – Ongoing inflammation, especially neuroinflammation, can disrupt acetylcholine production

- Certain medications – Antidepressants, antihistamines, and anticholinergic drugs can block acetylcholine activity

- Aging – Natural aging can lead to declining acetylcholine levels, affecting memory and muscle function

GABA

GABA is the only inhibitory neuropeptide, acting like the brake pedal to slow your brain down. All the others are excitatory or stimulating to the nervous system.

Diet: Foods rich in glutamate, the precursor to GABA, can help. Try:

- Fermented foods (kimchi, yogurt, kefir)

- Green tea (contains L-theanine, which promotes GABA activity)

- Bananas, almonds, walnuts (contain magnesium, which supports GABA function)

- Leafy greens (spinach, kale, broccoli)

Exercise: Regular physical activity, especially yoga and aerobic exercise, has been shown to increase GABA levels.

Meditation & Deep Breathing: Mindfulness practices can enhance GABA production and reduce stress.

Sunlight Exposure: Vitamin D plays a role in neurotransmitter balance, including GABA.

Herbal Supplements:

- Valerian root: Known for its calming effects

- Passionflower: May enhance GABA activity

- Ashwagandha: Helps regulate stress hormones and supports GABA function

Dosages & Considerations

- L-theanine (from green tea or supplements): 100–200 mg per day

- Magnesium (from food or supplements): 200–400 mg per day

- GABA supplements: 250–750 mg per day (consult a healthcare provider before use)

- Herbal extracts: Dosages vary, but typically 300–600 mg for valerian root and 250–500 mg for passionflower

GABA:

This is a test for leaky brain (a break in the blood-brain barrier).

When you take a drug that stimulates GABA production in the brain, you inhibit your inhibitions, start to feel more relaxed, and if you keep consuming, you slow down, get tired, feel sluggish, and lose coordination. If you keep taking those drugs, you will lose consciousness.

Alcohol and Valium are probably the most famous GABA stimulators. If you have ever tried either, you know exactly what I mean.

Consuming GABA directly shouldn't do this. Alcohol and THC cross the blood-brain barrier; GABA does not. When we take GABA internally, we should not feel brain inhibition. There should not be a slowing, intoxication, or incoordination feeling. There should be no brain effect at all.

INSTRUCTIONS

1. About 1–2 hours after dinner, on a night that you have nothing planned, take the 2 GABA capsules.

2. Notice any unusual slowing-down-type feelings, ranging from mildly intoxicated, uncoordinated, lethargic, or simply slowed down.

3. Notice any excitation, agitation, or other stimulation such as feeling wired, which will happen in approximately 20% of the cases of compromised BBB. Most will feel inhibited.

4. Go to bed. If you feel slowed, it will be gone by the morning.

5. **Any** change—excitation or inhibition—is a positive test for damage to the blood-brain barrier.

6. If you have a positive test, don't get a vaccine containing mercury or formaldehyde!

The GABA challenge is crucial after concussion or TBI to confirm if leaky brain still exists.

GAD65 antibodies (GAD65-Ab) can impact brain function by interfering with GABA (gamma-aminobutyric acid) production, which is the brain's primary inhibitory neurotransmitter. Since GAD65 is responsible for converting glutamate into GABA, the presence of GAD65 antibodies can lead to reduced GABA levels, affecting relaxation and hyperactivity.

Effects on Relaxation

- Lower GABA levels can result in reduced inhibitory signaling, making it harder for the brain to regulate stress and anxiety.

- Individuals with GAD65 autoimmunity may experience muscle stiffness, anxiety, and difficulty relaxing.

- Conditions like stiff-person syndrome (SPS) and autoimmune encephalitis are linked to GAD65 antibodies, leading to excessive muscle contractions and heightened nervous system activity.

Effects on Hyperactivity

- Reduced GABA means less inhibition of excitatory neurotransmitters, leading to increased neuronal firing.

- This can contribute to hyperactivity, restlessness, and even seizure disorders.

- Some studies suggest that GAD65 autoimmunity may play a role in neurological conditions like epilepsy and cerebellar ataxia, where excessive excitatory activity disrupts normal brain function.

GAD65 antibodies (GAD65-Ab) develop due to an autoimmune response, where the immune system mistakenly targets glutamic acid decarboxylase 65 (GAD65)—an enzyme crucial for GABA production. This process is linked to various autoimmune conditions, including Type 1 diabetes, stiff-person syndrome, and autoimmune encephalitis.

How GAD65 Antibodies Develop

1. Genetic Predisposition – Certain genetic factors increase susceptibility to autoimmune reactions.

2. Environmental Triggers – Viral infections (such as Epstein-Barr virus), toxins, or stress may initiate immune system dysregulation.

3. Molecular Mimicry – The immune system may mistakenly attack GAD65 due to similarities between foreign pathogens and self-proteins.

4. Chronic Inflammation – Persistent immune activation can lead to the production of autoantibodies against GAD65.

5. Gut Dysbiosis – Imbalances in gut bacteria may contribute to immune dysfunction and autoimmunity.

6. Blood Tests – Can measure this.

Dopamine Deficiency

Dopamine deficiency can be caused by various factors, including genetics, poor nutrition, lack of sleep, chronic stress, sedentary lifestyle, and certain medical conditions like Parkinson's disease and depression. Environmental toxins, excessive alcohol, caffeine, and sugar intake can also negatively impact dopamine levels.

To naturally boost dopamine, consider:

- Protein-rich foods: Turkey, beef, eggs, dairy, soy, and legumes contain tyrosine, a key building block for dopamine.

- Probiotics: Gut health is linked to dopamine production, so consuming probiotic-rich foods like yogurt and fermented vegetables may help.

- Exercise: Regular physical activity increases dopamine levels and improves mood.

- Sunlight exposure: Getting enough sunlight helps regulate dopamine and overall brain function.

- Meditation & Music: Both have been shown to enhance dopamine release.

- Supplements: Velvet beans (Mucuna pruriens) contain L-dopa, a precursor to dopamine, but dosage should be discussed with a healthcare provider.

- Listening to music you enjoy—especially emotionally engaging or uplifting tunes—can trigger dopamine release in the brain's reward system. Genres like classical, jazz, rock, and electronic have been studied for their effects on mood and motivation, but the best choice depends on personal preference.

- As for which ear, some studies indicate that the right ear may be more involved in processing speech and logical information, while the left ear is more attuned to emotional and musical elements. This means that if you're looking for a stronger emotional response, you might try listening with your left ear.

Olfactory Brain Stimulation

Noxious smells can activate different brain regions, including those associated with emotion, memory, and sensory processing. Studies suggest that unpleasant odors stimulate areas like the amygdala, piriform cortex, and orbitofrontal cortex, which are involved in emotional responses and decision-making. The right hemisphere of the brain is often linked to processing emotional and sensory experiences, meaning that exposure to strong, unpleasant smells could enhance right-brain activity in certain contexts.

- Interestingly, research has shown that the brain can separately process pleasant and unpleasant odors, meaning that different regions may emphasize either the positive or negative aspects of a scent. This could be useful in understanding how odors influence mood, cognition, and even behavior. So smell noxious odors into the right nostril only.

Pleasant smells can activate brain regions associated with memory, emotion, and cognitive processing. The left hemisphere is often linked to logical reasoning, language, and analytical thinking, so stimulating it with pleasant scents may enhance focus and cognitive function.

Some research suggests that floral, citrus, and herbal scents—like lavender, rosemary, peppermint, and jasmine—can positively influence brain activity. For example:

- **Lavender**: Known for its calming effects, it may improve focus and reduce stress.

- **Rosemary**: Has been linked to enhanced memory and alertness.

- **Peppermint**: Can boost concentration and mental clarity.

- **Jasmine**: Associated with mood elevation and cognitive stimulation.

Studies indicate that pleasant odors activate the orbitofrontal cortex, which plays a role in decision-making and emotional processing. Additionally, scent-related memory recall is deeply tied to brain function. Smell through the left nostril only.

Homeopathic Remedies

They work on the principle of "like cures like", meaning that substances causing symptoms in a healthy person are used in highly diluted forms to treat similar symptoms in someone experiencing anxiety. These remedies are prepared through a process of dilution and succussion (vigorous shaking), which is believed to enhance their healing properties.

Each remedy is tailored to specific anxiety symptoms:

- **Aconitum Napellus**: Helps with sudden panic attacks and intense fear.

- **Argentum Nitricum**: Used for anticipatory anxiety and nervousness.

- **Arsenicum Album**: Addresses anxiety related to health concerns and restlessness.

- **Calcarea Carbonica**: Helps with overwhelming fear and breakdown-related anxiety.

- **Kali Phosphoricum**: Soothes anxiety caused by exhaustion and hypersensitivity.

- **Gelsemium Sempervirens**: Treats performance anxiety, trembling, and weakness.

Homeopathy for Managing Depression

- **Ignatia Amara**: Often used for grief-related depression, emotional shock, and mood swings.

- **Natrum Mur**: Recommended for individuals who dwell on past emotional wounds, struggle with forgiveness, and prefer solitude.

- **Aurum Metallicum**: Used for severe depression, feelings of worthlessness, and suicidal thoughts.

- **Kali Phosphoricum**: Thought to be beneficial for nervous exhaustion, burnout, and stress-induced depression.

- **Sepia**: Recommended for hormonal-related depression, such as postpartum or menopausal mood swings.

- **Cimicifuga Racemosa**: Often used for depression linked to hormonal imbalances, particularly in women.

Homeopathy for Insomnia

- Coffea Cruda: Used for insomnia caused by an overactive mind.
- **Nux Vomica**: Helps with sleeplessness due to stress, overwork, or stimulants.
- **Passiflora Incarnata**: A gentle remedy for restlessness and nervous exhaustion.
- **Aconitum Napellus**: Helps with insomnia caused by anxiety or fear.
- **Arsenicum Album**: Used for insomnia linked to worry and perfectionism.
- **Chamomilla**: A remedy for insomnia caused by irritability or hypersensitivity.

Homeopathy for Bipolar Disorder

- **Lilium Tigrinum**: Used for increased energy levels and extreme restlessness.
- **Cannabis Indica**: Helps with excessive talkativeness and racing thoughts.
- **Belladonna**: Recommended for violent and aggressive behavior during manic episodes.
- **Veratrum Album**: Thought to help with impulsiveness and lack of self-control.
- **Hyoscyamus Niger**: Used for paranoia and erratic behavior.
- **Ignatia Amara**: Often prescribed for depression linked to suppressed emotions and grief.
- **Aurum Metallicum**: Helps with deep despair and feelings of worthlessness.

Homeopathy for ADD

(Homeopathy focuses on remedies that help with inattention, difficulty concentrating, and mental fog rather than hyperactivity.)

- **Baryta Carbonica**: Used for individuals who struggle with focus, memory, and mental development.
- **Lycopodium Clavatum**: Thought to help with confidence issues, forgetfulness, and difficulty processing information.
- **Carcinosin**: Often recommended for individuals who have trouble concentrating and organizing thoughts.
- **Tuberculinum**: Used for individuals who experience mental restlessness and difficulty staying engaged in tasks.

Homeopathy for ADHD

(Focuses on remedies that help with hyperactivity, impulsiveness, and difficulty concentrating.)

- **Tarentula Hispanica**: Used for children who are constantly moving, restless, and impulsive.
- **Carcinosin**: Thought to improve concentration and memory while reducing hyperactivity.
- **Stramonium**: Recommended for excessive hyperactivity and difficulty controlling impulses.
- **Tuberculinum**: Used for children who struggle with focus and exhibit destructive behavior.
- **Hyoscyamus Niger**: Helps with impulsiveness, excessive talking, and difficulty sitting still.

Acupressure is often used as a complementary therapy for mental health conditions. Acupressure works by stimulating points to restore balance in the body's energy flow.

https://acupuncture.com/education/points

Acupuncture Point Location Summary I Use the Most

Anterior View:

1. **Yin Tang** – Midpoint between the eyebrows on the glabella.

2. **PC6 (Pericardium 6)** – 2 cun proximal to the transverse wrist crease, between the tendons of palmaris longus and flexor carpi radialis.

3. **HT7 (Heart 7)** – On the wrist crease, radial side of the flexor carpi ulnaris tendon.

4. **LI4 (Large Intestine 4)** – On the dorsum of the hand, between the 1st and 2nd metacarpal bones, at the midpoint of the second metacarpal bone and closer to the 1st.

5. **SP6 (Spleen 6)** – 3 cun directly above the prominence of the medial malleolus, posterior to the medial border of the tibia.

6. **K6 (Kidney 6)** – In the depression below the tip of the medial malleolus.

7. **ST36 (Stomach 36)** – 3 cun inferior to the patella, one finger-breadth lateral to the anterior crest of the tibia.

8. **LV3 (Liver 3)** – On the dorsum of the foot, in the depression distal to the junction of the 1st and 2nd metatarsal bones.

Lateral View (Head & Foot):

Anmian – Behind the ear, midway between SJ17 (posterior to the earlobe) and GB20 (in the depression at the base of the skull).

BL62 (Bladder 62) – In the depression directly below the lateral malleolus.

Posterior View:

1. **BL13 (Bladder 13)** – 1.5 cun lateral to the lower border of the spinous process of T3.

2. **GV20 (Du 20 / Governing Vessel 20)** – On the midline of the head, 5 cun posterior to the anterior hairline (or at the midpoint between the apexes of both ears).

Arm Detail View:

1. **LI11 (Large Intestine 11)** – At the lateral end of the transverse cubital crease, in the depression at the lateral edge of the elbow.

Conditions Treatable

Anxiety:

- **HT7 (Heart 7)** – Calms the mind and reduces anxiety.
- **PC6 (Pericardium 6)** – Helps relieve emotional stress and tension.
- **Yintang** – Located between the eyebrows, known as the "third eye" point for relaxation.

Depression:

- **LV3 (Liver 3)** – Helps ease depression and irritability.
- **SP6 (Spleen 6)** – Balances emotions and supports mental well-being.
- **GV24.5 (Governing Vessel 24.5)** – Located on the forehead, helps calm the mind.

Bipolar Disorder:

- **K6 (Kidney 6)** – Supports emotional stability.
- **GB13 (Gallbladder 13)** – Helps regulate mood swings.
- **LI4 (Large Intestine 4)** – Used for general relaxation and emotional balance.

Insomnia:

- **BL62 (Bladder 62)** – Helps with sleep disturbances.

- **HT7 (Heart 7)** – Calms the nervous system and promotes restful sleep.

- **Anmian** – A special point for treating insomnia and improving sleep quality.

ADHD:

- **GV20 (Du 20)** – Helps improve focus and mental clarity.

- **Sishencong** – Four points around GV20, used for cognitive function and concentration.

PTSD (Post-Traumatic Stress Disorder):

- **ST36 (Stomach 36)** – Supports overall mental and physical resilience.

- **LI4 (Large Intestine 4)** – Helps relieve stress and emotional tension.

- **HT7 (Heart 7)** – Calms the mind and reduces anxiety.

- **PC6 (Pericardium 6)** – Helps with emotional regulation and trauma recovery.

- **LI11 (Large Intestine 11)** – Used for balancing emotions and reducing agitation.

- **LV3 (Liver 3)** – Helps with impulsivity and hyperactivity.

Common Symptoms of PTSD:

- **Re-experiencing symptoms:** Flashbacks, nightmares, and intrusive thoughts about the traumatic event.

- **Avoidance:** Steering clear of reminders of the trauma, including people, places, or activities that trigger memories.

- **Negative changes in thoughts and mood:** Feelings of hopelessness, memory loss, and negative beliefs about oneself or others.

- **Hyperarousal:** Increased anxiety, irritability, difficulty sleeping, and being easily startled.

Lowering High Cortisol Levels Naturally

Here are some effective natural sources and their recommended dosages:

1. **Adaptogenic Herbs**

   - **Ashwagandha** – Helps regulate cortisol and reduce stress. Dosage: 300–600 mg per day.

   - **Rhodiola Rosea** – Supports adrenal function and lowers cortisol. Dosage: 200–600 mg per day.

   - **Holy Basil (Tulsi)** – Has calming effects and supports adrenal health. Dosage: 300–500 mg per day.

2. **Nutrients & Supplements**

   - **Magnesium** – Helps regulate stress hormones. Dosage: 200–400 mg per day.

   - **Omega-3 Fatty Acids** – Found in fish oil, reduces cortisol. Dosage: 1–2 grams per day.

   - **Vitamin C** – Supports adrenal health and lowers cortisol. Dosage: 500–1000 mg per day.

   - **Phosphatidylserine (PS)** – Reduces cortisol levels, especially after intense exercise or chronic stress. Dosage: 300 mg per day.

3. **Lifestyle & Diet**

   - **Dark Chocolate** – Contains flavonoids that reduce cortisol.

   - **Green Tea (L-theanine)** – Promotes relaxation and lowers stress.

- **Meditation & Deep Breathing** – Proven to reduce cortisol levels.

- **Regular Exercise** – Moderate-intensity workouts help regulate cortisol.

Raising Cortisol Levels Naturally

Here are some effective methods:

1. Diet & Nutrition

- **Healthy fats**: Avocados, nuts, and olive oil support adrenal health.

- **Lean proteins**: Chicken, turkey, and fish provide amino acids for hormone production.

- **Complex carbohydrates**: Whole grains like quinoa and brown rice help stabilize blood sugar.

- **Salt intake**: Moderate sodium consumption can support adrenal function.

2. Supplements & Herbs

- **Licorice root** – Helps prolong cortisol activity. Dosage: 400–800 mg per day.

- **Vitamin B5** – Supports adrenal function. Dosage: 500–1000 mg per day.

- **Vitamin C** – Essential for cortisol production. Dosage: 500–1000 mg per day.

- **Adaptogens (like Rhodiola)** – Help regulate cortisol levels. Dosage: 200–600 mg per day.

3. Lifestyle Adjustments

- **Morning sunlight exposure** – Helps regulate cortisol rhythms.

- **Moderate exercise** – Strength training and aerobic workouts support adrenal health.

- **Stress management** – Meditation and deep breathing can optimize cortisol balance.

How do you know without a test if you're running high or low?

- **Inability to fall asleep** = High cortisol.

- **Inability to stay asleep** = Low cortisol.

- **Belly fat** = High cortisol.

- **Face, back, and shoulder fat** = Thyroid-related.

- **Hip fat** = Typically too much estrogen.

Adrenal Cocktail

An adrenal cocktail is a nutrient-rich drink designed to support adrenal health, balance stress hormones, and replenish essential minerals like sodium, potassium, and vitamin C. It's often used to help with fatigue, stress management, and hydration.

Basic Adrenal Cocktail Recipe:

- ½ cup orange juice (for vitamin C)
- ½ cup coconut water (for potassium)
- ¼ tsp sea salt (for sodium)

Variations:

- Pineapple Margarita Mocktail – Swap orange juice for pineapple juice and add lime juice.
- Blackberry Lemonade Adrenal Cocktail – Blend blackberries with lemon juice and coconut water.
- Guava Adrenal Cocktail – Use guava nectar instead of orange juice.
- Sparkling Adrenal Cocktail – Add sparkling water for a fizzy twist.

Sex hormones play a major role in shaping brain chemistry, influencing neurotransmitter activity, cognitive function, and emotional regulation.

Here's how they impact brain function:

1. **Estrogen**

   - Boosts serotonin – Helps regulate mood and emotional stability.

- Enhances dopamine – Supports motivation and cognitive function.

- Promotes neuroplasticity – Encourages brain cell growth and connectivity.

- Protects against neurodegeneration – May reduce the risk of Alzheimer's disease.

2. **Testosterone**

- Increases dopamine – Linked to motivation, focus, and reward processing.

- Enhances aggression & competitiveness – Influences risk-taking behavior.

- Supports memory & spatial skills – Plays a role in cognitive performance.

- Regulates stress response – Helps balance cortisol levels.

3. **Progesterone**

- Modulates GABA activity – Promotes relaxation and reduces anxiety.

- Supports sleep – Helps regulate circadian rhythms.

- Influences mood – Can contribute to emotional stability.

4. **Cortisol & Stress Hormones**

- Interacts with sex hormones – Chronic stress can disrupt estrogen and testosterone balance.

- Affects neurotransmitter function – High cortisol levels may reduce dopamine and serotonin.

Sex hormones also influence brain structure, affecting regions like the hippocampus (memory), amygdala (emotion), and prefrontal cortex (decision-making).

Herbal & Supplement Support

- Ashwagandha: Helps regulate testosterone and cortisol.

- Maca root: Supports libido and hormonal balance.

- Shatavari: Beneficial for estrogen regulation.

- Vitamin D: Essential for testosterone and estrogen balance.

Phosphatidylserine (PS) plays a role in sex hormone regulation by influencing cortisol, testosterone, and dopamine levels. **300–600 mg/day**

Effects on Sex Hormones & Brain Chemistry

- Cortisol Regulation – PS is known to reduce cortisol levels, helping to balance stress responses and prevent excessive hormone disruption.

- Testosterone Support – Some studies suggest that PS may enhance the testosterone-to-cortisol ratio, which can support muscle growth and cognitive function.

- Dopamine Enhancement – PS helps maintain dopamine signaling, which influences motivation, focus, and emotional stability.

- Serotonin & Mood – By supporting brain cell communication, PS may indirectly improve serotonin function, aiding mood regulation.

Testosterone can influence cognitive function, but its effects vary depending on age, baseline levels, and individual health. Research suggests that optimal testosterone levels may support memory, focus, and executive function. However, increasing testosterone beyond natural levels does not necessarily enhance cognition for everyone.

Potential Cognitive Benefits

- Improved memory & focus – Testosterone may enhance spatial memory and executive function.

- Better decision-making – Some studies link testosterone to impulse control and problem-solving.

- Mood regulation – Balanced testosterone levels may reduce depression and boost confidence.

Considerations & Risks

- Excess testosterone can lead to aggression, impulsivity, and mood swings.

- Individual differences – Some people experience cognitive benefits, while others may see no change or negative effects.

- Age-related decline – Testosterone replacement therapy (TRT) may help older individuals experiencing cognitive decline.

Estrogen plays a significant role in cognitive function, but rather than having the "opposite" effect of testosterone, it influences the brain in different ways. Research suggests that estrogen supports memory, learning, and neuroprotection, particularly in women.

- Enhances memory & learning – Estrogen is linked to improved verbal memory and cognitive flexibility.

- Supports neuroprotection – It helps maintain brain plasticity and protects against neurodegeneration.

- Regulates mood – Estrogen influences serotonin and dopamine, which affect emotional stability.

- May reduce dementia risk – Some studies suggest early estrogen therapy could help prevent cognitive decline.

However, the effects of hormone therapy on cognition remain complex. Some studies indicate no long-term cognitive benefits when estrogen therapy is started later in life.

DHEA (Dehydroepiandrosterone)

- Acts as a precursor to testosterone and estrogen, supporting brain function.
- May enhance memory, focus, and mood.
- Low levels are linked to cognitive decline and reduced energy.

DHEA is commonly used for anti-aging and cognitive support, but safety depends on dosage, duration, and individual health factors. Here's what research suggests:

Recommended Dosage

- Most studies use 25–50 mg daily for cognitive benefits and anti-aging.
- Higher doses may be effective but increase risks of side effects.
- Starting with a lower dose (e.g., 10–25 mg) and adjusting based on response is advisable.

Safest Forms

- Micronized DHEA – Improves absorption and reduces fluctuations.
- DHEA-S (Sulfate form) – More stable and commonly tested in research.
- Bioidentical DHEA – Derived from natural sources like wild yams.

Potential Benefits

- May support memory, mood, and cognitive function.

- Helps combat age-related decline in brain health.

- Can balance hormones that influence cognition.

Risks & Precautions

- Long-term use may affect hormone balance.

- Not recommended for individuals with hormone-sensitive conditions.

- Consult a doctor before starting supplementation.

Progesterone

- Has a calming effect on the brain and helps regulate mood and cognition.

- Supports neuroprotection, reducing inflammation and aiding recovery after brain injuries.

- Low levels may contribute to memory loss, mood swings, and anxiety.

Thyroid Hormones (T3 & T4)

- Essential for brain development, metabolism, and cognitive function.

- Hypothyroidism can lead to brain fog, depression, and memory issues.

- Hyperthyroidism may cause anxiety, restlessness, and difficulty concentrating.

Fungal Infections

Fungal infections can have complex effects on neurotransmitter metabolism, including norepinephrine and dopamine. Some research suggests that certain fungal toxins may interfere with enzymes involved in neurotransmitter breakdown, potentially altering dopamine levels. Additionally, fungal infections affecting the central nervous system can contribute to neuroinflammation, which may indirectly impact neurotransmitter balance.

Certain fungal infections, particularly those affecting the central nervous system, can contribute to neuroinflammation and oxidative stress, which in turn may alter neurotransmitter metabolism. If fungal toxins interfere with enzymes like monoamine oxidase (MAO) or catechol-O-methyltransferase (COMT), it could slow the breakdown of norepinephrine into dopamine, potentially affecting mood, cognition, and autonomic function.

In conditions like Parkinson's disease, where dopamine metabolism is already impaired, any additional disruption—whether from infection or inflammation—could exacerbate symptoms. Similarly, fungal-related neuroinflammation has been explored in psychiatric disorders, including depression and schizophrenia, where dopamine and norepinephrine imbalances play a key role.

There's a lot to unpack here!

There are several natural antifungal remedies that may help combat fungal infections and support neurotransmitter balance:

- Garlic – Contains allicin, a powerful antifungal compound that may help reduce fungal overgrowth.

- Turmeric – Contains curcumin, which has antifungal and anti-inflammatory effects.

- Coconut oil – Contains caprylic acid, which may help fight fungal infections.

- Oregano oil – Rich in carvacrol and thymol, both of which have antifungal properties.

- Probiotics – Help restore gut microbiome balance, which may reduce fungal overgrowth.

- There is growing research suggesting that fungal infections, particularly Candida albicans, may play a role in neurodegenerative diseases like Alzheimer's. Some studies indicate that fungi can enter the brain, triggering inflammation and producing amyloid beta-like peptides, which are associated with Alzheimer's disease.

- Since fungi thrive in sugar-rich environments, excessive sugar consumption may contribute to fungal overgrowth, potentially exacerbating neuroinflammation and cognitive decline.

Hence, I prefer a carnivore or keto diet, eliminating most carbohydrates. Certain foods are known to boost brain function, memory, and cognition.

BRAIN-BOOSTING STRATEGIES:

- **Fatty Fish** – Rich in omega-3 fatty acids, which support brain cell communication and memory.

- **Leafy Greens** – Spinach and broccoli contain vitamin K, lutein, and folate, which help slow cognitive decline.

- **Berries** – High in flavonoids, which improve memory and protect against neurodegeneration.

- **Nuts & Seeds** – Walnuts, almonds, and pumpkin seeds provide healthy fats and antioxidants for brain health.

- **Dark Chocolate** – Contains flavonoids and caffeine, which enhance focus and memory.

- **Eggs** – A great source of choline, which supports neurotransmitter function.

- **Green Tea & Coffee** – Caffeine and antioxidants help improve alertness and cognitive function.

Food Colorings, Chemicals, and Metals Causing Mental Brain Issues

Reducing exposure to artificial additives, processed foods, and environmental toxins can support brain health. Some detox strategies and alternatives to consider:

Ways to Minimize Exposure

- Choose natural food coloring – Opt for products using beet juice, turmeric, or spirulina instead of synthetic dyes.

- Eat organic – Reducing pesticide exposure through organic produce may help brain health.

- Filter water – A high-quality water filter can remove contaminants, including heavy metals.

- Limit processed foods – Avoiding foods with excessive preservatives and additives can prevent potential neurotoxic effects.

- Cook with safe materials – Use stainless steel or cast iron instead of non-stick cookware that may contain harmful chemicals.

Potential Detox Strategies

- Increase antioxidant intake – Foods rich in antioxidants, such as berries and leafy greens, may help counteract oxidative stress.

- Support liver detoxification – Drinking water with lemon, consuming cruciferous vegetables, and ensuring adequate hydration help eliminate toxins.

- Boost fiber consumption – High-fiber foods like flaxseeds and psyllium can aid in removing harmful substances from the body.

Color Can Influence Memory and Learning, and Green and Red May Have Advantages Over Traditional Blackboards

Why Green and Red May Enhance Memory

- Green is associated with calmness and concentration, which can improve focus and retention.

- Red is linked to attention and alertness, potentially boosting recall for important information.

- Blackboards (which are often actually green) were originally used because they reduce glare, making them easier to read.

- Blue – Encourages creativity and productivity, supporting cognitive abilities.

- Yellow – Boosts energy and engagement, making learning environments feel more inviting.

Studies on color psychology suggest that contrasting colors can help with memory retention, especially in educational settings. Color plays a significant role in learning environments, influencing attention, memory, and emotional responses. Studies suggest that green and red can enhance memory and focus more effectively than traditional blackboards.

Music Affects Learning & Cognition

- Boosts memory – Listening to music can activate memory-related brain regions, improving recall.

- Enhances focus – Certain types of music, like classical or instrumental, can help maintain concentration.

- Supports emotional processing – Music engages the limbic system, which governs emotions and motivation.

- Improves brain plasticity – Musical training strengthens neural connections, aiding cognitive flexibility.

- Reduces stress & anxiety – Music can lower cortisol levels, helping with mental clarity and learning.

Best Music for Learning & Memory

- Classical music – Composers like Mozart and Bach are linked to improved focus and memory retention.

- Instrumental music – Music without lyrics helps minimize distractions while studying.

- Lo-fi beats – Relaxing, rhythmic beats can enhance concentration and reduce stress.

- Nature sounds with music – Blending music with natural sounds (like rain or ocean waves) can improve relaxation and cognitive function.

- Baroque music – The structured rhythms of Baroque compositions may help with problem-solving and logical thinking.

How Music Enhances Learning

- Boosts dopamine levels – Music stimulates the brain's reward system, increasing motivation.

- Improves memory recall – Certain melodies can help encode and retrieve information more effectively.

- Reduces stress – Calming music lowers cortisol levels, making learning more efficient.

- Enhances creativity – Exposure to diverse musical styles can inspire new ideas and problem-solving skills.

B Vitamins Play a Crucial Role in Learning, Memory, and Cognitive Function

Key B Vitamins for Learning & Cognition

- B1 (Thiamine) – Supports energy production and nerve function, essential for focus and memory.

- B2 (Riboflavin) – Helps with brain energy metabolism and reduces oxidative stress.

- B3 (Niacin) – Aids in neurotransmitter production and supports cognitive clarity.

- B5 (Pantothenic Acid) – Important for stress regulation and hormone balance.

- B6 (Pyridoxine) – Crucial for neurotransmitter synthesis, including dopamine and serotonin.

- B7 (Biotin) – Supports nervous system function and gene regulation.

- B9 (Folate/5-MTHF) – Essential for brain development, memory, and cognitive processing.

- B12 (Methylcobalamin) – Prevents brain shrinkage and supports nerve health.

Studies suggest that B6, B9, and B12 are particularly important for memory and cognitive function, with deficiencies linked to cognitive decline. Get the methylated forms.

Mushrooms That Boost Memory & Learning

- Lion's Mane – Stimulates nerve growth factor (NGF), promoting brain cell regeneration and improving memory.

- Cordyceps – Enhances working memory and learning capacity, potentially improving focus.

- Reishi – Supports stress reduction and neuroprotection, helping with cognitive clarity.

- Chaga – Rich in antioxidants, which may protect brain cells from oxidative stress.

- Maitake & Shiitake – Contain compounds that support brain function and immune health.

Minerals That Support Cognitive Function

- Magnesium – Essential for brain plasticity and memory formation.

- Zinc – Supports neurotransmitter function and learning ability.

- Iron – Helps deliver oxygen to the brain, improving focus and cognitive performance.

- Selenium – Acts as an antioxidant, protecting brain cells from damage.

- Copper – Plays a role in neurotransmitter synthesis, aiding memory retention.

For some people, a nutrient-rich diet is enough to support brain function. However, individuals with gut health issues, absorption disorders, or dietary restrictions may need supplements to reach optimal levels.

How We Learn – Different Methods Impact Memory

Each of these activities—reading, writing, touching, and listening—engages different parts of the brain and contributes to memory formation in unique ways. However, research suggests that multisensory learning, which combines multiple methods, creates the strongest memory patterns.

- Reading – Activates visual processing and comprehension areas of the brain, strengthening recall.

- Writing – Reinforces memory by engaging motor skills and cognitive processing.

- Listening – Helps with auditory memory and verbal recall, especially for language learning.

- Touching (Kinesthetic Learning) – Engages tactile memory, making concepts more concrete and memorable.

Which Is Strongest?

Studies suggest that writing and kinesthetic learning (touch-based activities) tend to create stronger memory patterns than passive reading or listening. Writing forces the brain to actively process and encode information, while hands-on activities help reinforce concepts through experience.

Phonics instruction lends itself to multisensory teaching techniques, because these techniques can be used to focus children's attention on the sequence of letters in printed words. As such, including manipulatives, gestures, and speaking and auditory cues increases students' acquisition of phonics skills. An added benefit is that multisensory techniques are quite motivating and engaging to many children.

How Brain Lateralization Affects Learning
Brain lateralization plays a significant role in learning and creativity, but it's more complex than the traditional "left-brain vs. right-brain" idea. Both hemispheres work together, but they specialize in different functions.

- **Left Hemisphere** – Handles language, logic, and analytical thinking, making it crucial for structured learning like math and reading.

- **Right Hemisphere** – Focuses on creativity, intuition, and spatial awareness, supporting artistic and imaginative thinking.

- **Corpus Callosum** – Connects both hemispheres, allowing them to work together for problem-solving and comprehension.

Impact on Creativity

- Right-brain dominance is often linked to artistic and innovative thinking, but creativity also requires logical structuring, which involves the left hemisphere.

- Music, art, and storytelling activate both hemispheres, enhancing creative expression.

- Problem-solving benefits from both analytical (left) and intuitive (right) thinking.

- The left and right hemispheres of the brain process information differently, but they work together rather than functioning independently.

Left Brain vs. Right Brain Functions

Left Hemisphere	Right Hemisphere
Logical thinking	Creativity & imagination
Language processing	Visual & spatial awareness
Analytical reasoning	Intuition & holistic thinking
Mathematics & sequencing	Recognizing faces & emotions
Detail-oriented tasks	Big-picture thinking

- Some people think they are "left-brained" or "right-brained." Research shows that both hemispheres work together for most cognitive tasks. The brain is highly interconnected, and functions like language, memory, and problem-solving involve both sides.

- Strengthening both hemispheres of the brain can enhance learning, creativity, and cognitive flexibility. Here are some effective techniques:

1. Cross-Lateral Movements

- Activities like dancing, yoga, and tai chi engage both hemispheres.

- Bilateral coordination exercises (e.g., juggling, playing musical instruments) improve brain integration.

2. Brain Training Games

- Sudoku, chess, and crossword puzzles challenge logical and creative thinking.
- Memory games enhance neural connections and cognitive flexibility.
- Word searches help the right brain, as do new faces and music with high pitches.

3. Meditation & Mindfulness

- Alternate nostril breathing is believed to balance brain hemispheres.
- Mindfulness practices improve focus and emotional regulation.

4. Creative & Analytical Activities

- Drawing, painting, and storytelling activate the right hemisphere.
- Problem-solving, coding, and math puzzles strengthen the left hemisphere.

5. Music & Sound Therapy

- Listening to binaural beats may help synchronize brain activity.
- Playing an instrument engages both hemispheres simultaneously.

6. Alpha Current Stimulation

- Specifically, transcranial alternating current stimulation (tACS) has been shown to enhance cognitive function by influencing neural oscillations. Alpha waves (8–12 Hz) are associated with relaxed focus, creativity, and memory processing.
- Studies suggest that tACS can modulate alpha activity, potentially improving attention, learning, and cognitive flexibility.

- You can do this through YouTube videos playing alpha binaural beats in the background, or get a machine (which I feel is INCREDIBLY useful).

  https://balmahome.com/product/the-original-ces-alpha-stim-therapy-device

Food Cravings

Food Cravings Can Be Fascinating

They are influenced by hormones, stress, sleep, and even habits.

Common Food Cravings and Their Meanings

Craving	Possible Meaning	How to Fix It
Chocolate	Magnesium deficiency, stress relief	Eat dark chocolate (80% cacao), nuts, seeds, or leafy greens
Salty foods	Dehydration, stress, adrenal fatigue	Drink more water, eat potassium-rich foods like bananas
Sugary foods	Blood sugar imbalance, lack of sleep	Prioritize sleep, eat fiber-rich foods to stabilize blood sugar
Cheese	Tryptophan deficiency, dopamine boost	Opt for hormone-free dairy or nutritional yeast
Ice	Iron deficiency (linked to anemia)	Check iron levels, eat iron-rich foods like spinach and red meat
Carbs (bread, pasta)	Low serotonin, emotional comfort	Eat whole grains, exercise to boost serotonin
Red meat	Iron or protein deficiency	Include lean meats, legumes, and nuts in your diet
Fried foods	Fatty acid imbalance, stress eating	Eat healthy fats like avocado, nuts, and olive oil

Craving	Possible Meaning	How to Fix It
Coffee	Caffeine addiction, low energy	Hydrate properly, get enough sleep, try herbal teas

Drugs Side Effects

Why Not Just Take Drugs?

Psychiatric drugs have evolved over centuries, with contributions from various scientists and pharmaceutical companies. The development of modern psychiatric medications began in the mid-20th century, with breakthroughs in antipsychotics, antidepressants, and mood stabilizers.

Key Figures in Psychiatric Drug Development

- **Henri Laborit (1950s)** – Discovered the first antipsychotic, chlorpromazine (Thorazine), which revolutionized schizophrenia treatment.

- **Roland Kuhn (1957)** – Developed the first tricyclic antidepressant, imipramine, leading to modern antidepressants.

- **Arvid Carlsson (1950s–60s)** – His research on dopamine led to the development of L-DOPA, a treatment for Parkinson's disease.

- **Paul Janssen (1960s)** – Created haloperidol, a widely used antipsychotic.

- **Eli Lilly & Co. (1987)** – Introduced Prozac (fluoxetine), the first SSRI antidepressant, which changed depression treatment.

Concerns & Controversies

Some critics argue that psychiatric drugs have been overprescribed and that pharmaceutical companies have prioritized profits over patient well-being. Concerns include:

- **Side effects** – Many psychiatric drugs have significant side effects, including dependency and withdrawal symptoms.

- **Big Pharma influence** – Some believe that pharmaceutical companies have marketed psychiatric drugs aggressively, sometimes downplaying risks.

- **Alternative treatments** – Critics argue that therapy, lifestyle changes, and holistic approaches are often overlooked in favor of medication.

Haldol (haloperidol) is a first-generation antipsychotic that can cause neurological side effects, but it does not literally turn someone into a "robot." However, some people experience severe movement disorders or emotional blunting, which might feel robotic. It's a popular choice here in Chicago.

Potential Long-Term Effects

- **Tardive Dyskinesia** – Involuntary movements that can persist even after stopping the medication.

- **Parkinsonism** – Stiffness, tremors, and slowed movement, resembling Parkinson's disease.

- **Emotional Blunting** – Some users report feeling emotionally flat or detached.

- **Neuroleptic Malignant Syndrome (NMS)** – A rare but serious reaction causing muscle rigidity and altered mental status.

While these effects can be long-lasting, they are not inevitable for everyone. But to take the chance of turning your loved one into a shuffling **ROBOT**—is it worth it? The debate over their long-term effects and ethical concerns continues...

Psychiatric Drug Trends and Impact

Psychiatric drug prescriptions—including sedatives, antidepressants, psycho-stimulants, and antipsychotics (psychotropic drugs)—keep soaring. Acts of violence and suicide may incrementally be increasing because of the massive increase in these prescription psychotropic drugs. In the wake of massive increases in psychotropic drug use in the U.S., the CDC reported that from 1999 to 2014 the suicide rate increased 24%.

"Did Antidepressant Play a Role in Navy Yard Massacre?"

Scientific American, 20 Sept. 2013

https://blogs.scientificamerican.com/cross-check/did-antidepressant-play-a-role-in-navy-yard-massacre/

In the United States, approximately **8.5% of children under 18** are on psychiatric medications, including:

- **1.2% of preschoolers**
- **4.3% of children aged 5–11**
- **12.9% of 12- to 17-year-olds**

The most commonly prescribed medications include ADHD drugs, antidepressants, antipsychotics, and anti-anxiety medications. The use of psychiatric drugs in children has been steadily increasing, with concerns about overprescription and long-term effects.

Concerns About Psychiatric Drugs in Infants

Some infants under 1 year old are prescribed psychiatric medications, including antidepressants, antipsychotics, and anti-anxiety drugs. Reports indicate that thousands of infants have been prescribed these medications, often for behavioral concerns such as aggression, excessive crying, or lethargy.

- **Lack of Clinical Trials** – Most psychiatric drugs have not been tested on infants, raising concerns about safety.
- **Brain Development Risks** – Experts warn that these medications may alter brain growth and neurological function.

- **Off-Label Prescriptions** – Many drugs given to infants are not FDA-approved for this age group, meaning doctors prescribe them based on judgment rather than established guidelines.

In the U.S., approximately **85,000 infants (0–1 years old)** were prescribed psychiatric drugs in 2020. This accounts for a small fraction of the total infant population, making it rare but still concerning. Are you kidding me!?

For specific drug classes:

- **Antidepressants** – Around 7,811 infants received prescriptions.

- **Antipsychotics** – About 1,318 infants were prescribed these medications.

- **Anti-anxiety drugs** – Roughly 60,068 infants were given these treatments.

- **Mood stabilizers** – Around 21,593 infants received prescriptions.

While these numbers are low compared to older children, the fact that thousands of infants are prescribed psychiatric drugs raises concerns about long-term effects and appropriate treatment approaches.

Some professionals argue that behavioral issues in infants should be addressed through non-medication approaches, such as parental support, environmental changes, and therapy.

Handing out drugs for a mental symptom without checking metabolites and toxins holds no more value than faith healing.

The journey toward optimal mental and physical health begins with understanding the tools at our disposal and the principles guiding our decisions. The decisions we make today have profound implications for long-term well-being—not just for individuals, but for their families and communities.

My Favorite Resources

Some of My Favorite Resources:

"If you did have a million-dollar racehorse, would you let him stay up half the night drinking coffee and booze, smoking cigarettes and eating junk food?"

... "Would you treat a 10-dollar dog or a 5-dollar cat that way? What about a billion-dollar body?"

— Zig Ziglar

Abraham Maslow, the psychologist best known for his Hierarchy of Needs—a theory that maps out what drives human behavior.

Picture a pyramid with five levels:

1. **Physiological needs** – food, water, sleep, shelter.

2. **Safety needs** – security, stability, health.

3. **Love and belonging** – friendships, intimacy, family.

4. **Esteem** – respect, recognition, self-worth.

5. **Self-actualization** – achieving one's full potential, creativity, personal growth.

Maslow believed we must satisfy the lower levels before we can focus on the higher ones. Though later research suggests we often pursue multiple needs at once, his model still offers a powerful lens for understanding what makes us thrive.

A significant portion of our mental health is shaped by our environment—both the physical spaces we inhabit and the social-emotional climates we navigate.

Physical Environment

- Noise, clutter, lighting, and air quality can all influence mood and stress levels. For example, natural light and organized spaces tend to promote calm, while chaotic or noisy environments can heighten anxiety.

- Urban vs. natural settings: Time in nature has been shown to reduce stress and improve mood, while overstimulating urban environments can increase the risk of anxiety and depression.

Social Environment

- Relationships and community are powerful buffers against stress. Supportive environments foster resilience, while toxic or isolating ones can contribute to mental health challenges.

- Workplace culture also matters. High demands, low control, or lack of support can lead to burnout and psychological distress.

Genetics + Environment = Mental Health

A recent twin study found that genetic sensitivity to the environment plays a big role—meaning two people can experience the same situation very differently depending on their biology. So while the environment is crucial, how we perceive and process it matters just as much.

MASLOW'S HIERARCHY OF NEEDS

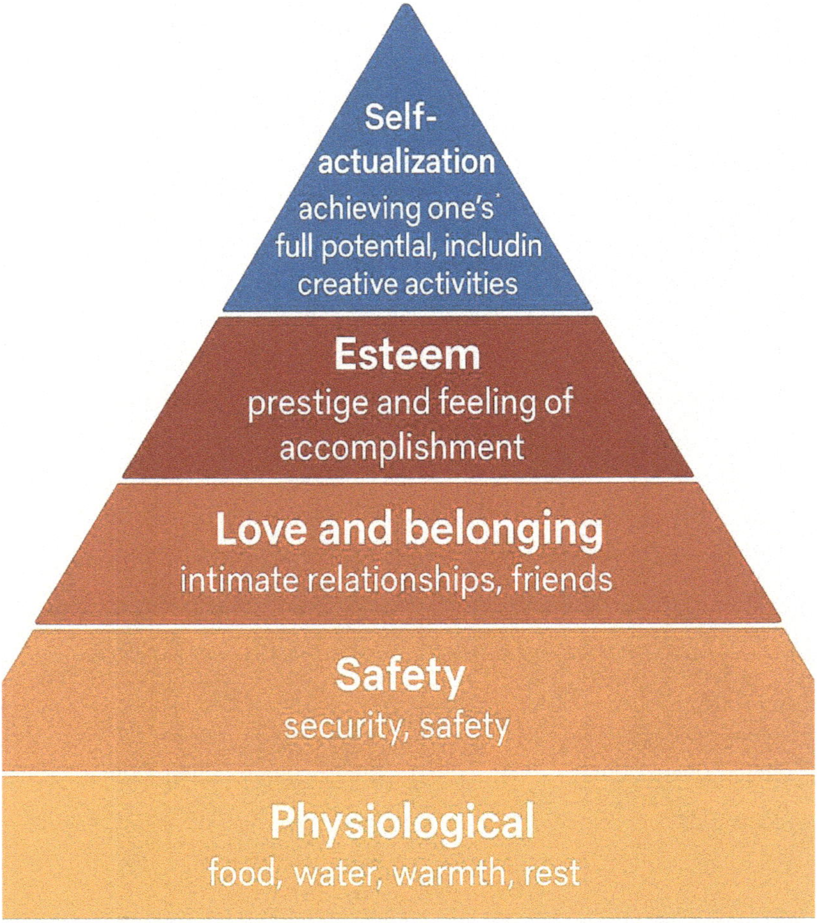

Kingdom Meditation (Inspired by the Gospel of Thomas)

Breathe in. Breathe out. Settle into the stillness beneath the noise.

"The Kingdom is inside you, and it is outside you."

"Bring forth what is within you, for what you bring forth will save you."

Now repeat to yourself, slowly and with intention:

- I am already whole.

- What I seek is already within me.

- The light I carry is not borrowed—

- It is original, ancient, and infinite.

- I no longer search outside for what lives within.

- I uncover. I remember. I return.

- I bring forth the truth I am here to live.

- In this moment, I walk in the Kingdom.

- It is not far—it is here. I am home.

Sit in that space for a few breaths, letting the words drift deeper than thought—into knowing.

Quantum Physics Perspective:

While psychologists may tell you about the laws of attraction, I find it does not work for some people. Have you heard that "opposites attract"?

Let's find out why.

If you want something, you are pulling it from the environment. It's just not going to give it to you, as everything needs to have a balance. If the environment wants something, it pulls that energy from you. If you want something, you pull it toward you. If you don't want it, you push it away. Simple, right? It looks like this:

YOU	OTHERS
Want <<<<	**>>>Want**
Don't want>>>	**<<<Don't want**

So you can see—the more you want something, the more you can't get it.

Plus, it creates anxiety because that dream or goal is always distant.

The answer? We are taught happiness lies within three things:

- Power

- Security

- Sensation

But there is never enough, so you must become **insouciant**. Insouciant is an adjective that means being carefree or nonchalant in a way that might seem a little too relaxed. Think of someone who strolls into a serious meeting five minutes late with a shrug and a smile—that's insouciant energy.

Synonyms include **unbothered**, **nonchalant**, **untroubled**, and **easygoing**. It comes from the French word insouciant, which combines in- (not) and soucier (to worry).

Laugh at any problem. Realize worrying doesn't fix anything.

"He who has eliminated doubt and fear has every thought allied with power."
—James Allen, a British philosophical writer best known for his 1903 work As a Man Thinketh

The Subtle Art of Not Giving a Fck* is a brutally honest and surprisingly funny read. Mark Manson is the three-time #1 New York Times bestselling author of this. It isn't about apathy—it's about choosing what truly deserves your energy.

Here's a distilled guide to mastering that mindset:

1. **Clarify your values**: You can't stop caring about everything—but you can stop caring about the wrong things. Decide what actually matters to you (your health, your goals, your people), and let the rest fade into background noise.

2. **Challenge the Spotlight Effect**: Most people are too busy worrying about themselves to obsess over your every move. Realizing this is liberating.

3. **Practice saying no**: Boundaries are your best friend. You don't owe anyone your time, energy, or emotional bandwidth.

4. **Accept imperfection**: You're not a robot (well, I am, but you get the point). Mistakes, awkward moments, and failures are part of the ride. Shrug, learn, move on.

5. **Let go of control**: You can't control others' opinions, the past, or the future. Focus on what's in your hands—your actions, your mindset, your reactions.

And finally, there are only four solutions to any issue:

YOU	OTHERS
Win	Win
Lose	Win
Win	Lose
Lose	Lose

So you see, half the time in life you win. Half the time you lose. Can you think of any other options? If you're both winning, keep doing the same strategies. If either is losing, consider compromising—which, as you see, is 50% of life's decisions. Lastly, if you and the other aren't working out, just walk away. Stop fighting a battle you won't win. It's a hard truth.

The choice is yours, my friend. Good luck on your journey to peace, happiness, and health!

For any questions, please reach out to Dr. Jung: **john@ask-drjohn.com.**